THE ACID
KING

THE ACID KING

Maggie Abbott

Published by

Escargot Books and Music
Ojai, California

To my brother George W. Bambrough, MBE

PROLOGUE

1984

Virginia Water, Windsor Great Park. England – Saturday

Serene flute music oozed from an expensive stereo. The cerebral Indian tones permeated every corner of an enormous white room the exact center of which was occupied by a slender long-haired man in lotus position on a dhurrie rug. Though engaged in meditation, his eyelids flickered at the muted ringing of a phone in the next room, then his head inclined to listen to a low voice answering it. Pete Stebbings' curiosity about the call on his private line took precedence over any commitment to spiritual contemplation.

His middle aged cockney minder, Tony, walked tentatively into the room carrying a cordless phone for Pete's attention. Tony had been in faithful service to his former school mate since rock and roll sounded the siren call, and by the time Pete made him official butler, he had acquired the grace and tact of a ballet dancer without the feet and the face. He whispered that it was Maddy, calling from Los Angeles.

Pete put on a pained face but clicked his fingers and beckoned the phone towards him. Then he opened his eyes. He simultaneously scooped up a palm of pistachio nuts from a bowl near him on the floor and tucked the phone under his chin, casually picking apart the first nut. A supercilious smile matched the tone of his voice.

"Well, it's the Lady Madeleine visiting the colonies. To what do we owe...."

"Cut it out, Pete, you smug little bastard. I'm not calling to ask you for anything. I'm doing fine, the kid's fine, she was sixteen two months ago and that's not what I'm calling about either."

Pete took a slow deliberate pick at his teeth with the long nail of a raised pinkie finger, revealing a dull gold eye tooth. The memorable famous face was a study in rock nostalgia, pouting lips and cat's eyes still a perfect fit with the sharp Nordic nose and waving blond hair. The only reminder of father time was the map of wrinkles on it.

Pete removed the food particle and flicked it away. He knew Madeleine would not break the silence until he apologized. Or made a pretense at apologia, which was the closest he could get, but he was going to take his time, just to annoy the bitch.

The fragment of damp pistachio landed on the lapel of Tony's black butler jacket. He discreetly drew a clean folded handkerchief from his top pocket, scooped up the missile and flipped it onto the carpet, replacing the hankie with the same dexterity. Out of the corner of his eye Pete was aware of Tony's moves and used it as an excuse to smile.

"Alright, let's start again, then. Good morning, Madeleine, how are you and how is Charlotte, and I did send her a birthday present, you knew that."

"Yes, I did. I also knew you didn't pick it out, nor did you remember the date. Your highly skilled slaves take care of that kind of thing, they've got better taste than you. That's how I can tell. Oh, I hear you're raiding the Far East now for suitably obedient female staff. How is Ling Ling?"

"That's one of the Pandas, you cow. Her name is Ling Pai and for once I've got a woman who doesn't talk too much. She's also great at figures, so I'm richer than I used to be."

"Alright Pete, leave it be. I never should even attempt these conversations with you. I just couldn't resist telling you I found the Acid King."

Pete's expressive face stopped the chewing and grimacing, and dropped its gravity for a few seconds, frozen in response. Suddenly he seemed dwarfed in the large room.

"You what?"

"Met him by chance last night, at some club, and a group of us went to his hippie pad for a drink. It was like Lazarus rose from the dead. I haven't been able to sleep, and I'm catching a plane later today after a bunch of interviews. Obviously he doesn't want anyone to know who he is. He's got a phony name. But I had to tell you."

Pete had by now adjusted his face to register disdain at the news. He sat in silence for a moment.

"That bastard is still alive, huh?"

"Yes."

Another moment of silence as Pete thought of the lives ruined, left in the wake of the man's deceitful acts.

Finally he spoke, his words considered.

"That's a pity, isn't it?"

Without waiting for an answer.

"Thanks for letting me know."

Then Pete put down the phone.

CHAPTER 1

Inside his state-of-the-art handsomely equipped recording studio less than an hour later, Pete stopped trying to work on the lyrics for a new song, and submitted to the jarring interruption of his meditation. He'd been denying the assault on his peace and privacy. Now he couldn't concentrate on his work. Nagging ideas, bitter memories and a mounting sense of irritation were taking over. He hated not being in control. Now he felt driven to share the news with someone. Who else but his former best friend Barry Turnbull, the other victim of Mister X's drug deal gone wrong.

Pete punched two numbers on the wall phone and Tony's voice immediately answered on speaker.

"Er, Tony, no call from the record company then? Mmmm. Get Barry Turnbull on the phone will yer, we've got the number somewhere."

Pete's face registered the strain of remembering an image from that night he'd never forget. It was one of several horrors that burned in his mind when he opened the hatch on that particular subterranean area called sixties memories he had cut out of his biography. This one was King Leo sitting in Jeremy's high backed antique armchair, primly nursing his silver attaché case while the local constabulary slowly felt inside all the pockets of every jacket, trouser and coat they could find in the house, looking for evidence of illegal substances.

The dealer had just glibly persuaded the cops to keep their hands off his case of precious unprocessed film. It was outrageous. "I'm a filmmaker, that's my life's work in there, my movie, exposed film that would be ruined if you touch it," he'd purred and pleaded.

Everyone else in the room knew what was really in those foil-wrapped packages, but couldn't say anything without incriminating themselves. Jeremy had some morphine in his toilet bag but his rich dad and various physicians would be able to fix that.

When the local boys in blue brought out some pills and a small bag of marijuana from their search, Pete and Barry exchanged the same horrified look. Pete never forgot that look. It said exactly what he already knew. It was all over. They'd never get out of this. It was beginning real slow, but a life of hell was about to start for the boy rockers.

Pete shook his head free of the nasty recall. He dug around on the shelves flanking the stereo unit, pulled out some old audio tapes with handwritten labels and squinted at the titles, knowing what he was looking for. He dropped a tape into the player and punched the start button. An infectious sixties number one hit blew the room inside out in spite of the limits of its eight track recording equipment. Two male voices brayed out clear lyrics in close harmony. Peter's face softened into an affectionate smile. There was no bitterness in his memory of good times with Barry when they were London's most popular band.

***

In Pete's large country house kitchen Tony sat with a younger London lad in chauffeur's gray uniform. They were perched on bar stools at the kitchen counter chomping on their sandwiches and potato chips. In the background an elderly woman in an old fashioned floral pinafore was rolling dough in a leisurely rhythm.

"If the number's not in the rolodex and he's not listed anywhere in the whole of Northumberland, then we've got to look at the old phone books. I know the box they're in, Freddie. Finish that and we're going to the garage."

"Oh hell, Tony, I've got time off this afternoon, right after lunch," moaned the young dark man in a rich second generation east end accent not at all related to his Jamaican face.

"The answer to that, Freddie, is tough shit. Himself wants to make a phone call. We're here to facilitate that. Right now. Forget the rest of that sandwich."

"Don't be hard on the young man, Tony," said the old lady.

"Keep out of this, Mum. I have to train them around here. You just feed 'em and spoil 'em it seems to me."

Tony laughed when he said this, and slapped his mother playfully on the bottom, getting her chuckled approval. She was already placing shrink wrap round Freddie's unfinished sandwich.

"He's been waiting fifteen minutes already, you know he don't take excuses."

The intercom rang loudly on the kitchen extension.

"There he is, already wanting to know. You tell him, Mum, just that we've gone to the garage to get the old phone books, won't be a jiffy. And he's getting his favorite treacle tart for dessert tonight."

After leaving the garage and a surprisingly successful rip through the boxes, Tony decided to deliver the good news in person, and tapped lightly on the recording studio door before walking in, still holding the door handle. He raised a folded piece of paper between two fingers.

"Got the number now, guv. Want me to get him on the line for you?"

"No, I'll dial it myself," said Pete, reaching out for the number.

CHAPTER 2

The Rose Bowl, Los Angeles – Friday

Ann glared at the plastic glass in her hand, blaming it for everything that was wrong about this evening, then swatted a few looks of contempt around the large tent set up as a hospitality room for friends and guests of Swindon Lodge, one of the few rock stars big enough to fill the Bowl these days. This looked like backstage area B to her, containing a number of flashy celebrities and die-hard names from the seventies party set, most of whom were delighted to see her. Probably because they didn't know she'd been out of the loop just as long as they had.

She knew for a fact that the current A List were in a more secure area where the star held court, and she was already certain he'd not be visiting this sub-group, preparing herself to be mortified when she failed to introduce her companion, ambitious young studio guy, Craig, to her famous friend as promised. What a pointless evening. And she still had to face several hours of old Swinny's too familiar pop ballads delivered with that well-honed *joie de vivre* spreading intimacy to each fan throughout the vastness of the Bowl.

Why did she always do this? Bringing some prop instead of having the guts to go alone to an event. She could have attached herself to Swindon's manager when he'd called to offer her tickets, but he'd clearly stated two comps. Maybe it was a message, she'd thought, keeping the distance of time and their social separation where it stood, still sensitive about herself and her slow slide down from the top of the heap.

So for a fraction of a second that thought had stopped her from offering him one comp back—he might have jumped at that—and asking nicely to share his company, thereby joining the inner sanctum where she belonged. Used to belong. Everything was too big now, the sanctum now a glut of famous names who had never met Swindon before, cleverly congregated by their domineering press agents. In the old days such people were classified as liggers and starfuckers, and only close friends were back there drinking the best champagne out of proper glasses to toast the rockers before they hit the stage and took on the hungry hordes.

These days the hungry hordes were backstage, requiring tight security to keep the superstar's current group away from accumulated old friends and their too ordinary companions, but the door was always open for the new big stars he hadn't met yet. And the eighties was bulging with them, the big hair and shoulder pad set, inspired by Miami Vice, and recently branded by the heat of *Vanity Fair* and *Entertainment Tonight.*

Celebrity was a club where stars felt comfortable only around each other. It wasn't smart to be around people who couldn't afford to bring their own lollies. Stars were guarded like the crown jewels. Passes handed out to old friends and family folk which landed them in Area B, where Ann was now. Old darlings who had sagged into the L.A. cesspool and were no longer either useful or glamorous. Worn out by too much competition and excesses of low grade coke.

Only well-established importance or meteorite fame stamped a passport into this Shangri La owned tonight by Swindon, Teddy and the branded headliners, with their lean sleek agenda of couture, well publicized deals, and arriving big at awards evenings.

***

God she was sour this evening. She hated herself for brooding about the past. If she'd never come to Swindon's big event, this irritating nostalgia wouldn't be interfering with her peace of mind. Or at least her very long road to find peace of mind, which seemed to be taking as long as withdrawal from a drug habit. Not that she'd ever had one, but she did have inside knowledge of how hard they were to shake.

The monkey on Ann Stapleton's back was the high of being a popular success, and the bruising pain of losing it all and not being on anyone's A list any more. Her choice. A wise one but bloody hard on her pride, and now she'd ruined her progress by letting in another glimpse of the way things had changed. She'd have to drive down Sunset to The Shrine for a few hours tomorrow, she decided, and get her spirits back to normal.

Ann sipped at the empty plastic, caught the ready eye of a waiter, shrugged privately and reminded herself that she'd somehow have the last laugh, it usually worked that way. She wished there were at least two or three of the young club scenesters in the room, but she knew in their reverse snobbery they wouldn't be seen dead at a middle aged event like this. Anyway she'd be meeting them in all their defiant punk glory tonight at the *Lingerie*, so she accepted another refill of pretty good Chardonnay, let go of the evil shit and started to enjoy this scene. She'd already hugged and done the tra la la with everybody in the room she knew.

Now she smiled at Craig, who was doing the neck exercise. Peering in all directions at the people in the room and sizing up the ones he wanted to greet. Ah, there was one. He excused himself and went off to talk to the young woman she recognized as the next big wheel at Paramount. Ann enjoyed the moment because she knew both Craig and the girl were guaranteed to be important studio moguls very soon and would qualify for the A room. They had the dedication. Ann only had the vision, not always a friend to her. Now she settled into her favorite pastime. Observing while sipping, never mind the container.

CHAPTER 3

Outside the tent, set apart from the huge number of fans sauntering around the grounds before concert time, some people in a group at the backstage VIP entrance were still vocally presenting their case to be allowed in. Vince Axle, a huge young hunk in security uniform, remained impartial but reasonable, explaining that the unfortunate ones either didn't have a pass at all, which was an easy one to argue, or that they might have expected to get a pass, or even been promised a pass by some poseur, but their name wasn't on the list, and the list was final. Which caused a lot of moaning and counter argument.

When a tall elegant woman arrived at the entrance, pardoning herself with enough authority to part the crowds, there was more grumbling. A man who'd been quietly standing behind the guard came forward to greet her.

"Miss Raleigh. Good evening."

"Reggie! Well, how nice to see you. Still here, then?"

"Yes, that much is the same. I was looking out for you. Come on in."

"Thanks, Reggie. Nice suit."

"Hey!" called out one of the frustrated. "Thought you said there's a list. Why're you letting her in?"

"You don't know Madeleine Raleigh, dude, you don't know rock and roll," said Vince, playing his best line of the night. He loved this job.

Inside the crowded tent, Ann was back in good spirits again, giving a witty commentary to

Craig as she pointed out some of the former luminaries getting into party mood with plenty of good wine and enough nibbles to make up for the obvious fact that Swindon was nowhere to be seen yet. Perhaps the more cynical among them had got the picture by now. Swindon Lodge was not coming to join the lowly, there was too much fun going on inside, with the latest hot young actors from the Coppola and Hughes stables, all telling great yarns, their loving babes in awe.

With her view of the entrance into the tent, Ann spotted Madeleine immediately and lit up in recognition before everyone else in the room did. It was probably that which drew Madeleine's attention to her, as she came over to Ann, smiling broadly, arms already extended wide for a hug.

"Now this is the A tent. Here comes royalty," Ann whispered to Craig, who turned to watch Madeleine's approach.

The two women embraced in the center of the room, under the gawking eyes of those who knew they were witnessing a newsworthy reunion. Madeleine stepped back, still holding Ann's arms, and examined her old friend minutely.

"Good God, girl. I never thought I'd see you again. What are you doing in L.A.? And you look so good. I thought I was the only old hag who could hold a light to these modern day groupies."

"Well, we've still got the legs, dear," said Ann, laughing at the ease and familiarity of sharing a time joke with someone who really knew her. "And if you seriously expect an answer to your question, it's another question. You free for dinner?"

"Yes, I am," laughed Madeleine, now turning her attention politely to Craig, standing there patiently, and blatantly impressed.

"And this is Craig Portman. Craig, Madeleine Raleigh, legend and survivor of the sixties revolution." She grinned mischievously at Madeleine, Reggie now behind her, politely hovering with a laminated pass in his hand, wanting to take her into the A room. "Craig is New Hollywood."

"Don't worry, Reggie. I'll have a drink here first. Tell Swindon I'd love to see him, though. You remember Ann Mayberry, friend of Swinny's." Madeleine winked at Ann, letting her know that she'd observed the stick-on pass Ann had fiercely slapped on her jacket.

"Yes, I do," said Reggie, shaking Ann's extended hand.

"Hello, Redge. Lovely to see you again. You're doing a wonderful job here. How is he? The boy genius."

"Better than ever. You'll see."

"Can't wait for the show. Say hi from me."

Reggie nodded, quickly found Madeleine some wine and headed off to report to headquarters.

"It's great to meet you, Madeleine. And I insist on taking you both to dinner at Le Dome. I have a reservation," said Craig, in the manner born to a climber who knew how to stay in the right niche once he'd found it. Madeleine and Ann mutually agreed by exchanging lifted eyebrows in subtle communication.

"Alright, that'd be very lovely. Thank you, Craig. As long as you don't mind being bored to death with an evening of nostalgia and very dirty stories," said Madeleine. "Then you can tell me what you did with the Old Hollywood. They never liked me. And by the way, that revolution. We lost."

***

All eyes shifted to the perception of action from a far corner of the tent. It was Swindon emerging from the inner room behind a guarded flap. He was flanked by three busy eye-swiveling minders, but he managed to spot Madeleine and Ann, clearly his mission, and created his own path through the gushing peasants, his laser beam of fame cutting a swathe as he wagged his precious arms vivaciously towards them both.

The rock idol jutted his famous head by way of greeting them, without a word, just gestures of camp delight, a life-long performer, playing out his intimacy with the women. He planted kisses on Madeleine's cheeks first.

"Darling old Swinny," she smiled. "I'm really happy you invited me, honestly, but how the hell did you know I was in town? I barely knew myself."

"Bloody good press agent, dear," he said to Madeleine, while pecking Ann's cheeks. "He knows all the tricks and don't think he doesn't overcharge me for it, either."

"Oh, shut up about your wallet, Swindon. I think you keep your brain in it," laughed Ann, giving him a little pinch on the thigh.

The star giggled like a fan, enjoying the rare luxury of being chided by someone who loved him but wasn't intimidated by his power.

"And you're still a bitch. So who are you two having it off with these days? Anyone we know?

Not this young man, I presume?" Swindon threw a horny wink in Craig's direction.

"No and no, Swindon. This is Craig Portman. You'll be able to make a movie deal with him one of these days, so remember the name. He's far too ambitious to be having it off with the likes of me. As for Madeleine, we only just met up again in this room. Ask her."

"Yes, what's your story, Maddy?" chuckled Swindon. "If you can trim it down to two minutes. Ann, I know you're writing for some independent rag, political as you ever were, no doubt?"

"Not really, darling, I just write my acerbic opinions about what's wrong with mainstream entertainment. It's a stunningly full time job, which makes me still something of an anarchist, I suppose."

"And I, dear Swindon, am about to launch a new CD of cynical songs for middle aged broads who've been dreading the arrival of 1984. It seemed easier than writing a book. I'll send it to you. If you listen to the lyrics you can pretty much catch up with my entire life since I stopped being Pete Stebbings' dolly bird of the year. Even penned one about our beautiful daughter."

"Daughter? I didn't know you had a kid together."

"No one does, it was the smartest thing I did, making sure of that. I protected her and made it easy for him at the same time. I was playing into his skinflint hands but it was more important that a little girl didn't grow up unloved and confused. I told him when she turned twelve. Now she gets expensive gifts. Frankly I prefer it this way."

"Sounds like a cynical song to me, sister," said Swindon, looking genuinely sympathetic and reaching out to hug Madeleine. "And after all you've been through, you really don't look like a tough old bird at all," he said, rocking her in his arms. Then he almost shoved her away, clicked his fingers for the waiter to bring over more wine, and chucked her tenderly under the chin.

"Now don't go feeling sorry for yourself. You and 'er," he said, cocking his head over to Ann with a lopsided grin. "You and Miss Ann here had the two prettiest boys of the entire century. I could never score either of them."

He grinned back at them over his shoulder as he sailed off into the waves of worship, shorter than everybody, but king of the room.

CHAPTER 4

Le Dome Restaurant, Los Angeles

Ironically they got a better table, in the back room, because the Maitre d' knew Ann, not on account of Craig's reservation. In fact, Henri merely gave Craig a lofty glance. He just beamed at Ann, touching her arm possessively as he guided her proudly past all the other diners, knowing they had spotted Madeleine Raleigh, something of a rock and roll Greta Garbo to the cognoscenti, who were well represented here tonight.

It was a buoyant occasion, with someone from each table in the small room knowing Ann and recognizing Madeleine, with a wave or a greeting. Others were peers of Craig, development types and hot young agents, so the table repartee was barbed and humorous. Food took second place as Ann noticed how many times short-term absentee diners came back from the bathroom together with that icy glow.

It surprised her that so many people were still doing cocaine. She really thought in her high-minded way that once she'd given it the bye-bye everybody else must have. Or should, judging by some of her old mates here tonight, where the cutting edge was showing a bit too close to the throat.

Most of them had been to see Swindon tonight, some in the private room with him. But Ann knew enough of the diners had seen Swindon hanging out with them at the Bowl, so she was quite pleased to relax and show off a bit. Instead of feeling regretful and ironic, it was easier to just enjoy being promoted back to her former popularity for the evening. It was a full hour or more before Ann and Madeleine could talk to each other.

***

"So what happened to that great career of yours, Ann? Last I heard you'd shipped out to L.A. with a bunch of glam stars under your arm."

"Ah. Was it a career? I never intended it to be, just doing a great job for a good salary, enjoying life and every adventure I could say yes to. But that was in London, after my poor old hubby died and I discovered the glories of independence. In Hollywood, when I settled here, it was suddenly serious. Deadly. I used to wake up every morning, pre-dawn of course, with a feeling of deep dread in my solar plexus. Well, to cut it fairly short, I got lured into a studio production company just at the moment when I was ready to give up being an agent-nanny defender of my territory." She drained her glass.

"The jungle was getting to me, not my kind of lifestyle at all. It was less a creative management kind of role and more like world war three, where I had to be constantly on alert to hold on to my successful clients, rather than just getting them great jobs, doing my all and having a life. And the clients couldn't be trusted, they enjoyed being seduced by killer shark agents, and I got more anxious and insecure. I knew it was a loser's game, on my own, without a big agency to bite back."

"And did you do the studio thing?"

"Oh God, yes, it was worse. I hadn't counted on the jealousy. Then through a power fluke I became a studio executive, and I could feel the loathing, more from inside the studio than outside. I was given a rare push up the ladder, and secret enemies were rampant, the toadies, attentive while you're up and willing you to go down. I received all the champagne, flowers, invitations to just everything, and tried to do a good job. I've never read so much—book manuscripts in boxes, and scripts, piles of them all over the bed, everywhere."

"Anything good?"

"Yes. We bought one, and it was mutilated into a piece of mediocrity. Don't let me stay on the subject, it was one disaster after another. I'd never had the training for that kind of backstabbing. I made all the wrong moves, picked controversial or argumentative projects to back, got elbowed out of the good ones. It's not self-pity, honestly, these were skilled professionals at the game. I was outspoken and naïve about the consequences, terrible combination. My hectic business days in London seemed by comparison like a duchess giving tea parties. But we got so much done then, we were still achievers. And our crowd made some miraculous films."

"Yes, it was a bit late for you to change your personality, not counting the years of course, just your accumulated experience."

"Well, both, I don't mind. I was always older than the artists and younger than the executives. I felt it was time to honor my own self. Acknowledge the fact that there were surely other more rewarding things to do with my life than trying to compete with these kamikaze masters. I had no idea what, having been in the entertainment biz for so many years. When I reached my explosion point, after a couple of years in the studio, and that embarrassingly bad movie on my résumé, I felt like I'd been banished from my own garden."

"What a horrible thought."

"Yes, my show business playground was suddenly packed with obnoxious kids playing for power and perks. I had to force myself to leave a familiar life that I loved, just to get away from them, and wander off to some unknown wilderness."

"Boy, I hope you're writing all this down. So you quit?"

"One morning I'd been crying after my producer finished yelling at me—someone's pulling my chain, he kept saying—I just got into my little AMC Pacer and drove off the lot for the last time. I felt like we were flying away, the relief and freedom were so immediate."

"I heard you got fired," said Craig, who had ingeniously drifted back to their conversation when his ears picked up a few key words.

"I'm sure you did. You heard it from the school of thought which advocates simple solutions like that. The rumor crowd. Someone said on TV that gossip is the official sport of the industry, and sex is the official hobby. No, I didn't get fired, they didn't have time and I didn't have anything to get fired from, thanks to timid lawyers. I looked at the state of the nation and I abdicated."

Madeleine turned to stare mockingly at Craig. "See? You're meeting all the queens tonight."

Ann's face lost the strained look and creased up into merry laughter. She nudged Craig affectionately.

"We warned you what our table talk would be like. Now it's her turn, so Madeleine, while I was being so damn successful what were you doing and where?"

"Funny. I was thinking that your years at the top were no better than mine at the bottom. It's all school, isn't it? Some of mine is not fit for young ears," laughed Madeleine, tweaking Craig's nearest lobe. "It's a lot about bad things like drugs, which are so trendy now it's a joke. When I was a junkie I was automatically an outcast. Now junkies are in an all-star cast of tabloid drama for the masses. Fortunately I did it all after the baby was born, and thanks to my dear old mum, my daughter grew up without seeing me at my bloody worst."

Madeleine yanked the bottle out of its bucket and filled Ann's glass then hers. Craig declined.

"My short sad marriage to Sir Timothy, lost soul, gave my daughter a name, gave me some borrowed dignity while shopping, and sent me off into a deeper abyss than my tragic drug crash after breaking up with Pete. I also scribbled down every one of my desperate thoughts in the form of poetry, now song lyrics. Then the cruel treatment I handed out to myself brought my voice down to this weird something which seems to hit the right nerve with the kids. You'll hear it all on my next CD. I should have called it Croaking the Wisdom. They're starting to promote it now."

"Yeah, it's called 'Yes She's Still Here'. I heard the single on KCRW last week, I loved it," said Craig. Far from irritation at being pushed around by these two women, Craig was showing an interest. It was that internal development boy instinct, Ann supposed.

"Ah, thank you. Good news. The title song's the only one I borrowed, answering the question before it gets asked. Like, 'Madeleine Raleigh! Didn't she die?' Corny but couldn't resist it. All the other songs I wrote. I'm proud of them, truthfully. I'm entitled to a bit of self-patting on the back because I see it as a triumph over where I was for years and years."

"There was another husband in there somewhere, also dead now, and a few well-chosen lovers. Chosen for their ability to fail me. There were three small movies I made even smaller with my crushing presence, one of which you got me, and the last one I got kicked out of. I made a couple of concert comebacks after I got off drugs, but that required a lot of drinking, then of course it was back to the drugs in the wake of my embarrassing performances."

"Yes I saw you once. At the Hollywood Palace. You were wearing a very crumpled black pantsuit. No blouse. There was a large safety pin doing a bad job of concealing that excessive cleavage from your fans in the balcony."

"Christ, yes, a vivid reminder. I can take it. When you're a junkie you don't have much time to think about clothes. Or anything really. Just how and when and how much you can score. It's a full time job being on the shit. Recovery, more than ten years later, is a glorious thing. But I still like a few glasses of wine when the company's good. I don't drink on my own any more. I bought a

Champion Juicer. I think I turned my skin quite orange from carrots at the beginning."

"Takes dedication. I did the clean-out too. Let's not talk about colonics."

"Let's not. Shouldn't we be off to that club of yours?"

"Just about perfect timing," said Ann, noticing that their host had already paid the check with his credit card. "You're coming too, aren't you, Craig? There's plenty of people watching there. It's a late night crowd."

CHAPTER 5

Club Lingerie, Hollywood

Parking was a challenge but Ann had been club-hopping for a long time around L.A. so she knew a few tricks, and on the three-block walk to the club they were able to observe some intriguing sights as groups of young people strolled alongside them on their way to the small front door only faintly illuminated by a subtle curly overhead neon sign.

Madeleine and Craig stood by and watched Ann magically weave their way in, with a quick check and a nod at the front desk, jumping the line, greeting a few people around her, and ending with them all being firmly stamped on the back of the hand with a small purple emblem. She was not only a regular but press, so she had privilege, playing it with modesty and easy friendliness.

"Hi Rage," said Ann to the tall cadaverous young man who controlled the door into the club. His face was a white powdery mask dramatized by a column of coal black hair rising like a crown above the heavily made up eyes. He bent down to kiss her affectionately on the cheek, and she casually introduced her friends. "This is Madeleine, and Craig. Full house?"

"As ever. It's the break before the main band comes on."

When they walked into the club only Ann was casual about the sight before them. It was packed wall to wall with people, not one of whom looked at all ordinary. The look was definitely punk but with dozens of variations, the girls were very young, mostly wearing black, there were teenage Dracula widows, red lipped angels with Nazi insignia, one with an SS cap worn with a comic tilt, skinny orphan wraiths, plump beauties showing pearly white skin through skimpy black lace bodices, there was green hair, purple hair, bright yellow streaks, and not one copy cat.

Craig's eyes had popped open to full extent and a leery smile was getting ever wider as he turned his head to take it all in. He was getting no reactions from his stares, only a sophisticated boredom, or an insolent stare-down. But amongst the crowd there was a vital and infectious camaraderie. It was as if this were home to the city's drop-outs, abandoned waifs, pirates, punks and lost souls, the look was moody but the underlying feeling was happy and expectant.

The canned music was hot, comfortably loud, and growing anticipation spread through the crowd as a handful of black-dressed roadies prepared the small stage, set against a plain brick wall, with slow but pleasantly involved concentration.

"Man," said Madeleine in Ann's ear, with a big grin. "This place is loaded."

"Yeah, quite an atmosphere, isn't it? This is the club scene, L.A. style. It's happening all over town. These kids have got it all worked out. They've invented themselves. Wait till you hear some of their names. See that girl over there with the cornrow do? That's Tequila. Tequila Mockingbird. And if you look around you'll see a nice-looking boy with really blue hair, he's Reuben Blue. He makes a monthly magazine for the scene, called 'Scratch', stapled pages full of

Xeroxed polaroid pictures of these characters, it's
fun. He chronicles every event, show, party, and
it's making stars of all these characters. Hollywood
can get stuffed outside of this world."

"The young men are surprisingly attractive
for such a raw lot. I just saw one with no top on,
just a couple of leather straps, and when I spot
him again I want to get a closer look at those
tattoos."

"Oh, he won't mind, he's very proud of
them. He's a lot sweeter than he looks, check out
the tattoos on his head. That's Ron, good friend of
mine."

"Do you know all these people?"

"Yes, I write about them in my weekly
column sometimes. If you're thinking hunky, check
out the band, it's The Red Hot Chili Peppers,
they're just wonderful. I'd take you backstage, but
here that's a skuzzy little room jam packed with
friends and fans, and they'll be coming out any
minute. In fact, here they come, look at the cheeky
one with tin cups on his shoulders. Everything's
original with this crowd. That's Flea," she grinned.

The noise drowned out the sound but
Madeleine's astonished face registered her mouth
saying "Flea??"

While the crowd surged forward and
concentrated their heat on the band, Ann flicked
her eyes everywhere, looking for a face, knowing
that Madeleine's attention wasn't on her. In spite
of the huge turnout for a popular local band, there
was someone missing, and Ann wondered why.

The band was so strong, confident and
unconditionally adored by the crowd that their set
was a nonstop blast of enthusiastic joy all round.
The time passed in a short whirl, with excitement

and approval written on every face. Here and there people were dancing, alone or together, some were walking around in the back, it seemed like there was a Corona and lime in every hand. It resonated as the best place to be in town and Ann was happy to see how much Madeleine and Craig were reacting to the scene, loving it all.

When it was over they drifted to the backstage room, only because Madeleine insisted on meeting them, it was a riot in there and they didn't stay long in the crush. Madeleine got what she wanted, including acknowledgement from the band, who knew enough about their rock and roll history to see this was Pete Stebbings' legendary girlfriend, checking her out with leery boyish smiles.

When they arrived at the car, Ann could see that Madeleine's face was flushed with excitement, and Craig was still tingling like a dowser.

"Hey, what do we do now? I'm not ready for sleep", said Madeleine. "There's still time for a drink somewhere. Anywhere fun we can go?"

"Fun. Let me think. Well, there are a few bars and clubs, but not much different from this one, and we'd have to face the parking hazard all over again. I've got an idea though. There's a funny guy I've been working with, well sort of working with and sort of funny. You'd have to see for yourself. He has a brilliant mind, bursting with provocative research, quite nuts but very amusing, he conducts a nightly pot party for the hip. I don't know why he wasn't there tonight, he usually is. I'd be interested in your take on him actually. It's sixties acid survivor in a young punk ghetto. Quite a standup comedy act when he's in good form.

And I'm writing a story on him for the paper. Which he doesn't know about yet."

"Is he a lover?"

"No. There was one time but I had to apply instant amnesia to the situation. He swept me up and it was obviously a big mistake because afterwards I got hit in the face with a huge emotional wall. I didn't want to give him up, and I've learned that in this jungle if you find someone delightful and they adore you back you don't let sexual confusion interfere with it. I've never spent a boring moment in his presence, but his antics are manic driven and sometimes he loses it. Recently he got so impossible to deal with I've been ignoring him. He'll put out the welcome mat. Let me make a call and see what kind of scene he's got going on."

"Scene? Hey, are you trying to scare me or invite me?"

"Madeleine, dear, you've always made it sound like the same thing. No, nothing antisocial, it's just that when he gets depressed he's no fun at all. I can tell the minute I hear his voice. So let me make the call."

CHAPTER 6

Griffin's Place – Fairfax District

There were four other people in Griffin's dark domain when they arrived. The atmosphere was light party, lots of stupid big grins from the two men whom Ann knew from other visits, one a lawyer turned poet, the other an up and coming comedy writer; they got a strained smile from a pretty teenage punk girl who probably looked her best when scowling, and an unfriendly greeting from a tense glamorous middle aged woman Ann had never seen before but knew to be Griffin's ex-wife Juno. They'd obviously been smoking a joint or several and had some snorts because there was a definite buzz on.

Ann knew it was worth a visit, just by the way Griffin had answered the phone, in mid-sentence, flying high and saying the first thing he thought of as a greeting. She could imagine the sly look he'd thrown at his audience as he told her to come right over. New visitors to spice up the scene. Griffin was the ringmaster of his little circus. Ann knew there would be more characters dropping in once the clubs closed, and so did he.

When they walked in Ann introduced Madeleine and Craig by their first names, but Griffin didn't pay attention to the details, he was too much in the moment, continuing to entertain his personal crowd, who rearranged themselves and their chairs under Griffin's direction so the new arrivals could have front row seats. They still had to listen hard to catch the surfer wave Griffin was rolling in on. Ann enjoyed the process and glanced at Madeleine to see that she was peering at him with interest, clearly finding his intelligence level and quick dance with vocabulary worth her attention.

Juno left noisily while everyone was shifting positions and there was no encouragement from Griffin for her to stay or to make much of her departure, just a grazing of cheeks on the way out.

Craig had placed himself as close to the punk girl as he could, but after a few whispered exchanges, glared on by Griffin, they had settled for watching him until the heat was off. Everyone was drinking just water, except Griffin, who sipped from a colored glass, concealing the syrupy intoxicant in there. He occasionally invited people to try some, in a manner indicating that to decline his expensive liquor would be appreciated by the host.

Madeleine had discreetly turned down the shade of a nearby lamp in order to seek the shadows but Griffin pinned down her gaze as he displayed his erudite knowledge and whizz-bang repartee, obviously intrigued by her and not allowing anyone else to share her orbit with him. He was doing everything in his bag of tricks to focus her attention on him, so it seemed like a corny gaffe when he nodded wisely, staring at her through narrowed eyes, and uttered.

"You remind me so much of a beautiful woman I once knew."

Madeleine wasn't helpful. Just waited for more of the same.

"You have a similar…look. I met her in Europe. You've been in Paris?"

"Of course."

"It's so long. You could really be her."

"Who?"

"Madeleine Raleigh, it's your eyes....."

Madeleine broke her mood and laughed merrily.

"Well that is funny, darling, because I am Madeleine Raleigh."

Ann just happened to catch the unguarded moment on Griffin's usually controlled features. Like he'd seen a ghost. Imperceptibly, shock and horror ran across his face like a flash of lightning, then he immediately recovered his cool in time for Madeleine's amused scrutiny.

"I don't remember meeting you in Paris," she said.

"It wasn't Paris."

"Where then?"

"Follow me."

When the music stopped, other conversations opened up, with Ann listening to the writer, so she missed Griffin's move, until spotting him in the dusk, guiding Madeleine to a far area of his one room apartment, showing her something on the wall while whispering intimately.

Madeleine was getting a memory from a sweet early place in her past. It came on like a cinematic flashback as Griffin flicked on a cigarette lighter and waved the flame briefly to give her a better look at the framed photograph.

It was quite a portrait. They were all sitting in a big tree, showing off for the camera. London's main swingers, vintage 1967, which at the shutter's click was still a very good year, but not for much longer. Caught them in the rapture of their first real acid experience. She remembered with sharp detail how very deeply happy she felt being with the friends she loved most and seeing fresh flowers after being in the London winter so long. In her memory a close-up of buttercups and vivid green abundant grass flashed the first hint of psychedelic in their bright spring colors.

For a hallowed moment she was back in the same state of bliss that filled her almost twenty years ago. She saw her own hand, framed by a floppy lace cuff, picking off a stem and adding the flower to her bouquet. She remembered lifting it to Pete's nose as he gave her that wonderful grin.

Looking over at that handsome face she thought she'd never forget, her bright voice came out of some big space.

"Hey! King Leo. When does it start working, your stuff?"

He was leaning against a tree. Playing with a cigarette, icy blue eyes dancing, and a knowing smile.

She watched herself, a young Madeleine, reaching her arms into the air with sheer joy and letting the bouquet fly high and free as the lysergic acid so seductively took over her senses. The flowers wandered down from the cool blue sky, tinkling like stars, birds joining in the laughter, everything so clear, including their young faces. Five guys and herself, a palette of beautiful youth, plentiful hair, velvet pants, reptile boots, hats, feathers and scarves, merging into a joyful surge as all six senses called in their response.

It was their last really happy day. They were all smiling, glowing, gliding through the grass. No music. Just the super deep sound effects of being in the loving soft embrace of nature. And him, the American geezer, taking the photo, someone Justin met in a club, a medicine man with some magical new drugs, who called himself the Acid King.

CHAPTER 7

Back in the dimly lit corner of his cave Griffin leaned closer against the wall and peered into Madeleine's face to get a reaction. She ignored him.

In her memory she heard his words, "You'll really feel it when we get to this place I found," as Leo sauntered off and led the way across another meadow. The Pied Piper and his happy child disciples skipping along behind him.

Next thing the whole group was climbing in the limbs of a big spreading oak tree, new leaves sprouting. Scrambling like kids to locate the right perch and arrange a theatrical pose.

Now all Madeleine could do was keep staring at the photograph. A montage of innocent lives floating in the big old tree. For one last second the image still sparkled with the charisma of the three most famous young media darlings of sixties London and their elegant friends. Then it was just an old black and white photo she'd never seen before.

She remembered him watching their faces all the time, silently chuckling in a sly kind of way, pleased with himself. The snitch who set them up and sold them out.

Now he was standing beside her, doing that same thing. She felt mesmerized, her whole body held in a spell, waiting for the hate to shoot to the surface like bile.

After a few moments Madeleine turned away from him, and walked back to Ann.

"Time we left, I think."

Griffin rushed over hoping to stop them.

"No. Stay. Here's a blanket, you'll catch a chill."

"Thank you," said Madeleine, sweeping up the steps as she threw the blanket around her again like a cloak. She grabbed the door handle and gave it a strong pull.

"No, I didn't mean..."

"Oh, I thought you did, and you can't change your mind now, can you" she said, grand and cold as the arctic, aware that Griffin was following her anxiously.

Ann waved nicely to the people left in the room, and beckoned Craig who was only torn away from his growing connection to the girl by the priority need to be driven home at this late hour.

Poor Griffin, thought Ann, watching him take the beating, stunned and confused as Madeleine and his precious blanket *walked* away down the alley. This was a vulnerable Griffin, a new face for the joker. She was still annoyed with his attention to Madeleine and was glad, for a change, to be leaving, wondering what happened.

Madeleine couldn't wait to get into the car.

"Ann. I want you to promise me that you will never see that man again," she said, closing the door.

"Why?"

"Because that's Mister X."

"You must be..."

"I'm not. That's him."

The young studio dude, exhausted from tagging along all night, went blank during this exchange. It meant nothing to him; he just wanted to lie down and sleep.

"What did you say to him?"

"Are you kidding? I didn't say anything. It took me what felt like ten minutes to pull myself together before I could act cool enough to make an exit. Look, I suddenly knew this was the legendary Leo, the man who changed all our lives. The man Fleet Street dubbed Mister X."

Madeleine paused at the drama of it. Ann was speechless.

"We blamed ourselves for being so stupid. None of us knew who he was, he just turned up through the grapevine with his little aluminum attaché case full of the best drugs only the inner circle could have access to. Barry said he brought the devil into our lives. We drove ourselves crazy trying to work out what happened, who did it to us and why. He couldn't have just been the lone ranger. How did he get in with us and how did he get out of the country?"

"My God. That explains so many strange things about Griffin. I'm still trying to take it in. Don't forget I never actually met him back then but I was included in all the talk about the bust. It was Justin and Tarquin he met first, he worked on them, told them about his pure acid, and they couldn't wait to introduce him to Pete and his circle, always wanting to impress them. Tarquin never got over the guilt, you know what happened. Justin's still around you know, he was made of harder stuff. His daddy wasn't such a brute as Tarquin's father."

"How the hell did you meet this man— Griffin he calls himself?"

"A semi-professional blind date. What else would it be in L.A.?"

"And you fell for him?"

"Are you surprised? He was so well informed and erudite, and he knew how to make me laugh like a silly teenager. I guess I've been in the Hollywood desert too long."

"I suggest we take Craig home, then go to your place where you can tell me more about this story. I'm intrigued and completely wide awake."

CHAPTER 8

Ann's Apartment, West Hollywood

"Yes it was probably the laughter, and the shower of brilliant non-stop references he tossed at me. I felt like a lead cloak had been lifted off my shoulders."

"So it was a sweet old mind fuck from the start. He hasn't changed since 1967. Good thing you never met him back then."

Madeleine and Ann were drinking tea now, in Ann's apartment off Holloway Drive, having dumped the sleepy guy, and eager to continue their investigation.

"I was the Monday morning quarterback, knew all about him but never saw his face. He's been very clever all this time, no slips, no clues. Just that old black magic. He's always playful, fun. Got my brain working again, you've no idea how boring most movie people are. And he had really nice grass. I couldn't tear myself away that first time. Never been so late for lunch in my life, and not the slightest bit sorry about it."

"You must have known he was doing a number on you?"

"I just enjoyed being swept off my feet. I thought, well, this could be my last love affair, it was not something I could turn down. It was like an act of fate, kind of irresistible. Wouldn't you do the same?"

"I would, I have, and I guess I will again. Must I imagine the rest?"

"Yes, because that's all I feel like talking about right now. I'm suddenly exhausted. What's important to me is how you turned up and changed everything."

"What puzzles me is this. He's obviously hiding his past, he never told you, so why the hell did he reveal himself to me? Just like that. He didn't have to, I didn't recognize him."

"Maybe he got carried away, suddenly seeing you, he's got a terrible ego. And he was seriously stoned."

"What are we going to do about this, Ann?"

"Oh, God, nothing I hope. I can't tell him I know any of this. I'll just lie. This night of revelations is too combustible. Pete mustn't know either."

"Course not."

"Why don't I believe you?"

"I feel vengeance, that's why. Just a little bit, but women do. We don't completely forgive the man who took us down the road into love and passion then suddenly snatched it away. Pete's it for me. I know Griffin did that to you. Drive him crazy stabbing him in his Achilles heel, and enjoy being the number one person in his life while you've got something he wants, just briefly, one more time, because he dropped the ending on you before you had the chance to do it to him."

CHAPTER 9

Whitley Bay, Northumberland - Saturday

The phone rang several times before the fat middle-aged man picked it up. He was slumped lazily in a shabby recliner, clicking a remote control over the Saturday sports programs on an oversize television screen, sucking back the last drops from a beer bottle. Hidden in this man somewhere was a once cherub-faced teenage hooligan, Barry Turnbull, an equal match for showy Pete Stebbings in the much loved sixties rock band, The Veils.

Barry was irritated by the interruption and made a loud barking hello noise at the caller, then sat up with a huge grin when he recognized the voice.

"Fuck me, Pete, it's you. How are you man? No, I changed it couple of years ago, no more Barry Turnbull, mate, anything for a quiet life, name's Barry Whiting now, the wife's moniker actually. Yeah, yeah, yeah, I'm okay, just don't ask, you know what I mean, life is what it is man, you know, fucking grind and all that."

Barry was reaching for a cigarette and gradually shifting to his feet, becoming more animated as he breathed some enthusiasm into his usual self. He was really happy to hear from his old, make that, former buddy, having no illusions about his low rank of significance in Pete's life.

"Better than rock'n' roll, eh? Howzit going man?"

Fortunately Barry was already inhaling nicotine and standing up straight when he heard the next part.

"Well, guess what, I had a call from our Madeleine just now."

"Oh yeah? Bloody Madeleine, surprised she's still with us, eh?"

"She was in L.A., doing some sleuthing. She found Mister X."

"What d'ya say? She what?"

"Yeah, The Acid King in person, alive and well and living in L.A."

"Jesus. Is that true? Now don't do this to me if it's not true, Pete. I managed to forget all that and now you bring it up again. I just feel the rage like it was yesterday. That's what me shrink tells me, she says I can't get the rage out of my liver."

Pete's face was expressionless, sphinxlike, as he listened.

"I thought God was taking care of all that for you, Barry."

"God? Oh, not now, mate. I gave that up, too many weirdos, all praying for the rent to fall out of the sky and fill up the gas tank on the way, you know what I mean, it's please Jesus for everything, utterly useless. Give me Freud, at least I can blame Mister X for my rage. I want to see that man dead every night when I can't sleep."

"How's your wife?"

"Carol? She's a tower of strength, I tell ya. Best day of my life when we got married. She's in the kitchen right now. Wanna...?....No. So how's yours?"

"Hey, don't ask don't tell, you know, but I can tell you, Barry, you've been a mate since whenever, nobody seems to know who I really am any more, or was. Life's great when you've got the right girl, but I just can't find her, makes for a fucking boring lonely life with all the wrong ones."

"Too bad, man."

I finally managed to get rid of the last one, Mrs. Money."

"You're right, it's boring. Besides man, this is England, it's all in the papers anyway. You know where he is?"

"In L..A. somewhere, she didn't say."

"You don't know? You didn't ask her?"

"Why would I? It's dead isn't it? Just had to share it with you, that's all. Barry, don't get worked up. It was seventeen years ago."

"So why are you bothering me with it, don't screw with me mind, Pete. I really don't need these downer phone calls from you. I still haven't recovered from the last one."

"Can't think what you're talking about, Barry."

Pete stood there, phone under his chin, arms akimbo, ready to back off, surprised at any kind of friction from old Barry, his loser buddy who always fed Pete's pride.

"The time you had the ego-sizzling problem with the tabloid and the false palimony thing and the chick attack you bent my ear with for a couple of hours. I love ya, man, but forget it. Just send me your CD's."

"And another five thousand pounds," said Pete.

Barry's face crumbled, relief and emotion in cahoots, his face creasing up with silent sobs, trying to hold them back.

"Thanks, Pete, you know I'm not asking for it."

"It's alright. I know," said Pete. "You never have. With you it's okay, you're the only one I can trust not to come on to me about anything. And this Mister X fucker, just forget about him, alright? Sorry I brought it up."

"I gotta go, Pete. I can't talk, please. Sorry I…I'll write you, okay?"

Barry put down the phone and dropped into his chair, heaving quietly. "Yeah, you trust me because I've got no power over you, I'm a nothing, I can't hurt you, you callous son of a bitch. I only tell you what you know already. But I'll take the five and I'll keep taking it whenever you offer it and I hope you never die, man, because I love you, you asshole."

Barry wiped his face with the back of his hand like a kid and recovered the ballsiness that made him a survivor. "Just bloody 'ope it's not another three years."

He hunched over the coffee table, splayed his hands and pounded a dramatic drum roll, calling out to the kitchen.

"Carol, hey Carol!!"

First he broke the good news to his wife, and checked out the roast, then Barry went to the bathroom for a session. After a while he tossed away the magazine and allowed his mind to wander.

Back to the time when he first heard someone knocking at the front door of Jeremy's cottage. They were all lounging peacefully in the drawing room, after a tiring day of dancing and prancing outdoors in psychedelic bliss. Now waiting for a delicious Moroccan feast beginning to beckon from the back kitchen where Jeremy's houseboy was doing his voodoo. Music was playing, it was Love, he remembered that, and as usual he was riveted by the action on a soundless television screen and how the movements sometimes synchronized with the music, kind of hallucinatory. Like the knocking on the door. He heard it but he thought it was the band.

Madeleine lay back in Pete's arms and he was playing with her hair. King Leo had placed himself in a throne-like chair, engaged in filling a hookah pipe. He didn't look up, just said to Jeremy, "Someone at the door."

"Oh, they're collecting money for the scouts, I expect," said Jeremy languidly, trying to get up off the big tapestry cushion.

James was already peering through the window curtain.

"It's actually a police constable."

"Always collecting, they are. Better give them something I suppose. Tell them I'll be one second."

"And some old geezer. God, my legs feel like water."

All the others in the room were examining James and Jeremy as if it were a scene in the school play. The upper class twits doing their best to be polite instead of ignoring the doorbell and staying in the groove.

Jeremy giggled as he lurched over to the entrance. By the time he got there, James was opening the front door, leaning on it for support and attempting to smile through the gap in a kindly way, while Jeremy offered a ten shilling note to a surprised constable.

Barry could never say exactly how it happened but the next thing he saw was that the room was full of coppers, including a couple of more senior types with different caps, and one blank looking chap in a raincoat. In his child-like imagination, enhanced by the LSD, Barry cheerfully thought he was still watching telly. Somehow he couldn't get past P.C.49 in his little mind. He had the uncanny feeling they were all equally slow at realizing that this in fact was a police raid, and the place was full of drugs, because nobody moved.

Except King Leo, taking advantage of the eyes of the law totally focused on the three very famous faces staring back at them. He swiftly and furtively got rid of the hookah under the chair, using a subtle move with his foot, and waited there with a newly blank innocent expression on his face.

That was why Barry was always convinced Leo had set them up. The cops deliberately ignored him, accepted his excuse not to open the telltale little case of drugs. They were either not interested in him because he was a nobody, or they knew exactly who he was and were told to leave him alone. Barry didn't have to wonder which.

In that instant the power of the acid caused Barry's infant state to skim back through past millennia of evolution and he watched himself become a raging primitive. The miracle which stopped him from jumping over to Leo and tearing out his throat like a jackal was the hand of Madeleine on his arm, digging in hard with her nails, restraining and reassuring him with dynamic strength whilst smiling sweetly up to the invaders.

"Good evening, officers. May I offer you some tea?"

CHAPTER 10

Pete's House, Virginia Water

Lying flat on his back and talking softly but clearly, Pete appeared to be having a conversation with himself.

"It was that guy who ruined my life. After the raid we got shat on in the papers and television news. Top of the Pops wouldn't take our new promo. Of course now it's a fucking classic, ha ha. We lost our new record deal and got stuck with the old one and a stinking ancient contract we signed when we were still doing pubs. As penniless criminals we had to drop the lawsuit against those middle aged Fagins. We could have broken that contract, but no money, no lawyer.

That was after they'd kept us in jail for two days and my best friend Barry was so ashamed and freaked out he had a nervous breakdown and went off his rocker. Not to forget my girlfriend became a junkie, my best mate killed himself and my manager went AWOL. You could never understand how it felt."

"I want to understand. Tell me more about how it felt."

Ling Pai was bent over Pete's ankle, carefully inserting an acupuncture needle into the skin, to join four others sprouting at different angles, and matching an arrangement on the star's other foot. She glanced up the long streak of white flesh that was Pete, her lord and master, and patted his thigh gently for reassurance.

"Go on."

"They were just the facts. How I felt was degraded. It was like losing my personality, like the real Pete Stebbings slipped away, my spirit. I managed to do some real play-acting in the slammer. Kept up my manly cockney patter with the guards and the other inmates who kept calling out to us in friendly support. I was one of them, yer working class bloke, yet they didn't object to my being the fancy rock star, that's what they wanted."

"I ordered up gourmet lunches and dinners on a tray covered with a white cloth, delivered by the local three-star public house. The waiters used to get cheers from the crowds outside the police station. We had our fans, and the press were there, taking pictures."

"We made front pages for days, then the headlines started up with 'Who is Mr. X?' and 'Where is Mr. X?' then 'Mr. X has left the country.' There was weeks of this before the trial and being put behind bars. We all went nuts trying to figure it out, discussing it on the phone with all our friends for hours, weeks. Everyone was talking about it. Couldn't get the fucker off our minds."

"Time to calm down and let the needles do their work," whispered Ling Pai in a soothing voice, like a familiar ritual.

On her knees she leaned over, laid her palms gently across his eyes for a moment, then stroked his hair. She quickly checked over the positions of all the needles and squeezed his hand.

"You should rest now. Relax your mind. I'll be back in a while."

Pete didn't bother to reply. She didn't expect it. Ling Pai was easy to be around. He sighed and tried a few deep long breaths like she'd taught him, to empty his mind, but there seemed fat chance of this. In his more relaxed state he could remember some of the bad scenes without the depression that used to go with them. That was a good sign.

It was easier to visualize the turning point out of his years of bad luck and remember events backwards from that. All it took was a freaky young guy from San Diego of all places who worked in a video store and had got himself hooked on Pete's one and only movie, the sixties underground collector's item, *Indigo Black*. In a movie industry declining into a split between overpriced hits and cheap indies, this geek managed to write and direct his first movie and make it a hit, with a Pete Stebbings original song on the soundtrack.

The song was an unknown track from a long ignored solo album Pete made during his seclusion in Jamaica. In spite of his devastation it had an upbeat lilt and a dance rhythm which had infused his sad solitary exile, helped along with God given ganja.

Pete's pursed lips relaxed into a satisfied smile as he remembered the way the tables turned. He got royalties, he got discovered and thrown into the limelight. He was perfect material for the late seventies, when disco was becoming a bore, here was the forgotten lead singer from a fractured band, sacrificed to the gods of war, a hero of a failed revolution. They saw him as a crushed flower child.

The media didn't get too much into the very old stories then, it wasn't time for the downer stuff; it was before the flamboyant television stars began to confess to the tabloids about drugs and incest. Pete confined his media confessions only to flashbacks of a naughty working class boy toying with glamorous sexy upper class girls, their outrageous clothes, make-up and hair. It was enough to keep the journalists busy, and hundreds of photographs came out of the files, setting off a feast of copycat looks, so Pete Stebbings became a new icon, with the character lines on his face a symbol of cool.

He felt contented with that last thought, and certain that in this world of the frenzied celebrity fan media industry, it would never change, he'd always be up there, legend, lover, star. He let it go finally and began to snore.

CHAPTER 11

Saturday

The next morning Griffin called Ann. It was very early, he couldn't have slept more than a couple of hours from the state he was in, his voice rough.

"What did she say, your friend?"

"You mean about you? Obviously, or you wouldn't be asking."

"Ann, that's cruel. I'm not like that. Not like other people you know. It's not all about me. You know that. I thought she was…a remarkable person. Well, she's a friend of yours. I wondered if she remembered that we met. It was a long time ago."

"She didn't say anything. We didn't have time, but knowing Madeleine she would have said something if it was important."

"Important?"

"I think she just wrote it off, you know, whether or not she met you. She's still sensitive about all the years she was out there on drugs, doesn't like to talk about it, she remembers very little from those bad times."

"So? You're not even curious?"

He knew her. Ann felt sharp currents warning her to hold back and lie.

"Not really, Griffin. If you like I'll grill her next time we talk on the phone. She's gone now, caught the mid-day direct to London."

"So let's forget it then. There's my other line. Next time."

He was gone. What a relief, thought Ann, hoping his paranoia was on idle right now, at least on the subject of Madeleine and their past, she'd done her best. It would be perfect to forget this whole incident happened, but she couldn't. She decided to do some research at the library, order all the books that covered the bust and do some prying of her own.

It was fascinating to her, almost two years of knowing and loving this man, and his secret turned out to be something that bound them more than he realized. He seemed to have no idea that these people were friends of hers too, nor her connection to Tarquin, if he even remembered him. Maybe because he wasn't at the weekend party. Her first real boyfriend, Tarquin, The Veils' upper class amateur press agent, who took the sickening bust of his dearest friends like a personal attack on his integrity, and lost everything, starting with her and ending with his own fragile life in a little sports car on the M1.

CHAPTER 12

Pete's House, Virginia Water - Sunday

Tony and his mother were in the kitchen as usual, having a sandwich lunch. The household budget made sure that these were first class sandwiches. Mum was just finishing with slicing the succulent whole ham on a bone. The Dijon mustard was standing by, with crisp lettuce and sliced home grown tomatoes on their separate plates. Tony was taking a healthy great bite out of his sandwich when Ling Pai slid quietly into the kitchen and sat down on a bar stool next to him.

"Can I talk to you, Tony?"

Tony nodded slowly, with a slight raising of the eyebrows and a quick glance at his mother, indicating with skilled practice that she should move out of earshot. He took his time to finish carefully munching on the delicious filling, knowing Ling Pai would politely wait until he had actually voiced his concurrence.

"Well it would be somewhat out of character, Miss Lotus Blossom, but talk away, do," said Tony after he had finally consumed the bite and flicked his tongue around inside his mouth to catch the good bits. There was no question where he had learned this technique of casual control.

"That man, Mister X, Pete wants him offed."

"Eh? Watch your mouth, girl. Where did you learn language like that?"

"I listen to him all day."

"Is that what he said? In those words?"

"No. He said it's what he used to want years ago. But he said something else. He said 'Will no-one rid me of this son of a bitch?'"

"Ah, now that sounds like the current Pete Stebbings, a well-read man, seen the right movies, and all that. So when did this occur?"

"It was yesterday, after that Lady Madeleine phoned and he talked to the man who was in the band."

"Barry? And you've been sitting on it all this time? To turn a phrase."

"He's been brooding ever since. Very unsettled. He was worse today."

"Can't say I hadn't noticed that myself. Well, thanks for bringing it to my attention."

Ling Pai and Tony sat there quietly for a minute, before she slid off the stool and started to leave.

Mum looked over from the fridge.

"Want a sandwich, dear? You look famished."

Ling Pai smiled no, and waved as she left the kitchen.

"Poor thing, she's too thin, never eats."

"Mum, she's built tiny, she's Asian, strong as a bull, solid as a rock, and very ambitious."

"I feel sorry for her. She works so hard to please him."

"It's a career she's chosen, Mum. None of our business."

"I agree with that, so be sure she doesn't make trouble."

Tony nodded and stayed deep in his thoughts for a while.

"Now you're brooding, just like him."

"So you were listening."

"No, I've just got good ears. I never ruined them at those loud rock shows, like you boys."

"What?" he shouted, cupping his ear.

They both laughed at their comfortable understanding of each other.

"I'm thinking of going up North for a trip. Drop in on old Barry. I'll get Freddie to drive me up, tell him we're giving the Jag a run."

"Hope you know what you're doing, stirring the pot."

CHAPTER 13

TWA Flight from Los Angeles to London - Sunday

Madeleine woke to that eternal hum of plane engines, and the gray morning light of the British Isles greeted her as she slid up the window cover. In her comfortable first class seat she'd managed to sleep since draining her dinner wine and now she cocked her ear for the first sounds of breakfast coming from the galley.

She'd dreamed for hours about the past. Only the last two minutes probably, but it seemed like an eternity as images jockeyed with memories, newspaper photos burned into her mind as if she'd witnessed them herself. Pete and Barry crammed into the back of a chauffeur driven car, still cheerfully waving to fans, not ready for the bad news to come. Another grainy photo, of the two boys being taken away in a police car, manacled, Pete's blurred grin still on show, Barry's head bowed, already beaten.

She'd also flashed on one of herself, rushing away from the cameras, long hair flying horizontally along with her scarf, big dark glasses, her young mouth clenched into a grim line. She'd stared for days at this picture of herself, took it as a symbol of her downfall. It was when the depression started, and she turned to the only comfort available to her. Heroin had been an adventure, now it became a crutch for her existence. She took it furtively at first, while she and Pete struggled to maintain their love affair but Pete was eventually disgusted by her obvious degradation, so she slipped away to die quietly somewhere dark and secret. A place where her famous face meant nothing, and she didn't have to be bright and charming.

In the following few weeks when she realized she was pregnant, Madeleine hid at her grandmother's cottage, forced to break from the drugs and allow the baby girl to arrive in good health. The loneliness of the cold rocky shoreline matched her pain. She pushed herself into utter misery and wrote down all her angry hopeless thoughts into piles of lined exercise books, hoping it wasn't true that the human fetus hears and absorbs what's going on outside of the womb.

CHAPTER 14

Griffin's Place

Griffin sat back in his deepest chair, the tiny lights and dark corners of his cavern surrounding him in a rare time of comfortable solitude. He finished mixing a cocktail of marijuana buds, and expertly rolled a joint, leaned back and inhaled with satisfaction, a tender smile on his face. Youth, innocence and mischief mingled in his expression, and peace seemed near at hand as the door burst open, revealing full daylight outside, and Juno thumping down the stairs. She flopped down in a chair as if it were home and put her hand out for the joint, taking a deep angry drag on it.

"So who were those women?"

Griffin took a profound breath as if patient and exasperated at the same time.

"Those two young ladies are in the business and could be helpful to my work. Why do you always get in the way when I have important contacts to take care of?"

"I didn't get in the way. I left, but you hardly noticed. And who's the English woman? She had a familiar face."

"Oh?"

"You didn't notice? Come on."

"They were both English. Names don't matter."

Juno sat there tightly wound and seething. Clearly this was routine.

"Do these business ladies know you have a wife?"

"Oh, I have a wife? Not exactly my preference. I'm still waiting for the divorce you keep postponing."

"Don't bullshit me, Lennie, you get what you want out of this arrangement, you always have. Speaking of which…"

"You're bogarting."

She passed him the joint, and picked up her bag. With a hard look at Griffin, she opened it, took out a piece of paper, unfolded it and made as if to hand it to him. As Griffin reached over for the check she pulled it away, smiling, and put it back in her bag. Then Juno calmly unbuttoned her shirt and started to strip off the rest of her clothes, starting with the bra that unveiled her breasts, full and firm, her whole body surprisingly erotic.

She stood proudly, and Griffin pushed past her, closed and bolted the door, came back and took hold of her breasts, squeezing and rolling them as he pressed hard against her, moved his hands down to envelop her buttocks and planted a deep throated kiss on her mouth. They were hot and completely naked in seconds, fucking each other, vigorous and noisy.

CHAPTER 15

Ann's Apartment, West Hollywood

Ann walked into her room and went straight to the answering machine, classic working girl style, starting to do other things as well as listen, but was stopped in her actions by the sound of Griffin's gruff rolling diatribe. From the resigned look on her face it was clearly not the first message in this tone she'd heard on her machine.

"Ann, I appeal to your warm heart, a woman who loves cats, you couldn't be so cruel, your silence is offending me. You hung up. No-one hangs up on me. No-one. What could I have done to turn you into a stranger? I would never hurt you. Nothing I have ever done was meant to hurt you. I know you want to talk to me. Please talk to me. Er, well, I guess you're not there. You know what you should do, Ann."

Ann shook her head as she waited for the next message.

"Ann, it's the Mad one. Here's my number, back in London….Got your message at the hotel, well you know that. Need to talk to you too."

Ann put everything down and picked up a pen, rewinding over the message to check the phone number, dialing it immediately. To her relief Madeleine's distinctive voice took over after one ring.

"Oh, Madeleine, it's Ann. I'm relieved to find you in. I was getting neurotic over this Mister X thing."

"Me too. You speak first."

"Well, I was worried because I never thought of insisting you keep this to yourself, especially not tell Pete or anyone in that circle, because there's that story on Griffin I never got round to telling you. He was involved in the murder, or seemed to be, of a very close friend, he's never recovered from the shock...."

"Well, I'm in the shit then."

"You didn't."

"Yes, I told Pete, couldn't help myself. But thank God he wasn't remotely interested. That's how he feels about his scandalous past, but you'll have to tell me more now you've started."

"His friend was shot to death when Griffin's car was hijacked. He went overboard with his guilt as well as the grief, as if he were convinced it was his fault. It didn't make sense at the time. It was very late at night, they'd been editing some music video, and Griffin was taking Billy home because his car wouldn't start, but he was sleepy so Billy was at the wheel. They were cornered by two cars in the middle of a dark street, one of the men just shot Billy in the head and dragged him out. Griffin made a run for it and the car was found the next day."

"I know what you're going to say."

"It suddenly struck me now you've told me who he really is that Griffin was the intended victim. This guy worked with him, in front of the cameras that Griffin hid behind."

"You think the people Griffin's hiding from tracked him down but got the wrong guy?"

"Yes. And it explains the mystery. Why he cracked up when it happened, not just mourning the loss of his friend, but paranoid with fear most likely because he knew it was meant for him, and he couldn't tell anybody, let alone the law. And that's why he took off like a coward and left Billy behind. When he saw they'd taken the car he called the police and went back there, but it was too late for Billy, and the mystery was why they left Griffin as a witness. He felt such remorse he took to the bottle on top of the coke and became a recluse after the funeral. He's obsessed."

"Oh-oh. I don't like the sound of that. You're worried that if word gets out, he's in danger of getting whacked for real this time?"

"How nicely you put it."

"Have you talked to him yet?"

"Not exactly. The last two days have become a bit crazy with him. It started okay because I just pretended you'd said nothing, but he got all worked up with the usual aids, obviously didn't get any sleep, and hit me with two weird phone calls in a row so I hung up on him, and I'm being persecuted for that. But I can read between his lines now. He's frightened. If his cover's blown he's got something to be scared about."

"We're safe. I didn't tell Pete a thing, didn't mention you either. But we do have to calm him down. Tell you what. This is my idea. Call him as if nothing's happened, say you just had a call from me, blah blah blah and I gave you a message for him. Say, 'She says remember that bit of old gossip you told her? Well, she promises not to tell anyone.' Then you've got to convince the guy that this means nothing to you, nor do you care. Try it."

"It's good. I'll put that into effect immediately. Before he starts his next round of nocturnal paranoid anxiety. I've never seen a frantic Griffin. Imagine living like that, poor man. It's the kind of life a coyote must have."

"Old Wiley Coyote. He can handle it. Just get him off your back with the same con he works on you and everyone else. He'll never know. Pete's forgotten it already, he's such a selfish sod since he got rich and famous again, it doesn't matter anymore. And now I can get back to my joyous life of promoting the CD. You'll see me in Los Angeles pretty soon when it's released there. Just let's stay well away from Him next time."

"You bet. I'm already easing away from him. He hates losing someone he didn't choose to excommunicate. And now I'm a friend of the stars again, in his eyes, he likes to show me off. He doesn't remember my Tarquin connection because he never met me then, and my name has changed, so that's a relief too."

"He's probably forgotten Tarquin anyway. He was just a support player, one of the club denizens, a stepping stone for King Leo. The big fish were his focus. Who would he have got busted next if there hadn't been such a hullabaloo in the papers? So are you going to be alright now? Will you call me if you have any drama and need help? You can just call this number, I pick up messages from anywhere. Good girl."

***

Ann took a huge breath and relaxed her shoulders after she put the phone down. Next stop was the fridge and an opened Chardonnay. She sank into a corner of the sofa, legs up, toes flicking off shoes, mind fully elsewhere.

She was working out how she could research the missing years in Griffin's life. She knew his real name from the book written about

The Veils, and she had seen a different one on his telephone bill, which she had accepted as his own. Griffin was so obviously an appropriate mythical image he had chosen for himself to have some power in the club performance world.

She needed to check out the office computer, see what it was capable of. Better still, go straight to the publisher's system, it had to be top notch in the field of research. On her second glass she felt confident enough to call Griffin and got the instant pick up, snappy response she knew indicated a bad mood.

"Hey, Griffin, it's Ann, what kind of message was that? Don't you understand deadlines? You know I have a serious job at the magazine, why do you take everything so personally?"

"You know I'm a sensitive person, Ann."

Griffin's self pitiful response hung in the air like an accusation and made her sigh.

"Oh, I also just got a call from Madeleine, she wanted me to know she was back in London and she had a message for you."

"Oh?"

"Don't ask me to explain what she meant, she said tell your friend that remember that bit of gossip he told me, I guarantee I won't repeat it. What does that mean Griffin?"

"Ah, well, just some sort of barbed joke about someone we used to know. Nothing really. Nothing." He let out a deep sigh. "Well, okay. Look I've got some people here, and...."

"It's okay, Griffin, I must get to sleep. I'll call you very soon. We'll talk."

Ann bounced back into the couch again and laughed with relief. It felt like a smooth ending, and she was pleased to see her affection for the man was dissolving. That was an improvement. She finished off the glass of wine and decided not to drink another one but go straight to bed and sleep.

CHAPTER 16

Barry's House, Whitley Bay

Carol and Barry were slumped at their kitchen table unit on vinyl chairs with matching tablecloth in a pale green mock tartan design, nicely coordinated with the teapot, cups and servers. Barry stirred his tea repetitively. Carol sipped at hers, lips pursed, eyelids blinking rapidly. She glanced up.

"I'm sick and tired of this, Barry."

"What about me? Howja think I feel?"

"I know how you feel. Don't you think I heard all about it enough for years and years? Over and over with your bloody vendetta. You wore me out. I can't start it up all over again."

"It's about you, then, is it? Poor you. Poor Miss Florence Fucking Nightingale. Didn't you get anything out of it? Look around. You did quite nice out of nursing this brain dead drunken rocker."

Barry stopped stirring, then quickly reached over and laid the hot spoon on the back of her hand.

"Ouch! You stupid git."

Barry cracked up, laughed and jigged around in his chair.

"Grow up."

"Maybe it's impossible for me to grow up. Ever thought of that? Could it be psychologically possible that I am forever caught in the warped mind of a juvenile jailbird. Eh?"

"I'm glad you're suddenly finding it funny. I haven't had any sleep for two nights in a row with your neurotic depression, and now you're trying to be humorous about it. What do you actually want, Barry?"

"Dunno."

"Come on, let's go upstairs, I'll give your back a rub, relax you."

Barry sat stonily. He needed to be persuaded. Carol was used to this. She got up and walked over behind him, starting to gently knead his knotted shoulders. He shrugged along with it, starting to melt a bit, then he felt for one of her hands and nodded towards upstairs.

CHAPTER 17

It was late gray afternoon when Carol woke up.

Her skillful hands had once again nursed Barry from tight shoulders to grunting orgasms and now he lay there beside her, eyes closed, fast asleep and certainly devoid of anxious thoughts for a short window of time. Carol gazed at him with resignation and other mixed emotions. She eased herself off her elbow, rubbing the stiffness out of it, and lay back on the pillow with a deep sigh.

Yes, she thought, I did alright. If you see this life as suburban Shangri La and not the end of the road, as she did. Her main regret was not having kids, therefore no grandchildren. That was bleak to her. They had argued about it so many times in the past, until the day she looked in the mirror and knew it was getting too late and thanked God for it, knowing Barry represented all the babies she'd ever know in her life to come.

By the time she'd accepted her lack of choices, the sadness of life had settled over her like a veil. She was profoundly lonely. There was no-one she could really talk to. Barry was his own planet and couldn't contemplate the invasion of someone else's thoughts. They exchanged facts about meals, the weather and constantly talked about what they did and what they watched on television. There was not much silence between then, but there wasn't any discussion.

That's what Carol missed. She wondered if she'd imagined it, worked hard at remembering. Yes, it was true, she had experienced that kind of conversation where you say something to a friend, and that person hears you and asks you to tell them more, so you elaborate on your thought, you extend the observation you made when you noticed something and your friend answers you and takes up the topic and you are both engaged in something that opens your mind, and it sings. Your mind sings. It's like brain adrenaline. It's called talking. Carol knew you couldn't just make it happen.

They had some neighbors who were friends, but they just cheerily exchanged the facts just like she and Barry. Not one mention of feelings, nuances of thoughts. Where would this dotty analysis lead her, Carol wondered. Maybe she should get a shrink of her own, someone to listen.

The nice butcher sometimes seemed like he'd be open to a bit of philosophy. She made a point of always going to his old fashioned little shop for meat and sausages, and bypassed that section in the supermarket. But one time Ray seemed to perk up his maleness at her interest in his chatter, and she backed away. She was afraid he had confused her bright-eyed eager enjoyment of his wit as a come on. Oh no, she couldn't allow that. Imagine if Barry caught a whiff there was a man she had even noticed. It would unleash the violent crybaby Carol had worked so hard to tame.

She kept away from the best pork bangers in the neighborhood for months so she could start with a clean slate, and settle the disappointment she felt at losing that little lift she'd always felt, being flirted with over the raw dead flesh. It was during that time that Carol saw the old film *Brief Encounter* on the bedroom television and cried bitterly, sobbing loud and free, knowing Barry was in noisy soccerland downstairs, sated on her best steak and kidney pie, shouting at the players and knocking back the beer.

That night was a turning point for Carol. That's when she realized what was over, what was left, and how to make the most of what she had. She blessed her guardian angels for the timing. Her niece's wedding was the following week, so Carol gave herself a complete makeover. Hair to toes, new dress, shoes and all. The stunning effect of her look and her apparent success in life as seen in the eyes of her older sister was the magic touch. She felt much better. Carol's relatives always remembered Barry as the legendary rock and roll star, proud of having him in the family. He had a ball singing old blues numbers round the piano at the wedding party, and everyone envied her.

Life had continued to be bland but not melodramatic anymore and Carol accepted that part of her was dead. But the part that was still alive was not bad. Not bad at all. And the sex was quite lively again, she always knew how to tweak Barry's buttons there and have the orgasm she wanted, even if she had to climb all over him to get it.

Now the ugly past had come back. The phantom who had caused the fall from grace of Barry and his band. That's what he'd become to Carol. A ghost, not a real person. A name, an image, an evil person, faceless and disappeared into the distance of times long gone and forgotten.

CHAPTER 18

At the sound of door chimes. Barry jerked into life, and Carol gently calmed him with her hand on his chest. She didn't want him to get up but he insisted, sleepy but master of his house.

"S'okay, I'll go."

As Barry approached the front door he saw two male heads behind the pebbly glass inserts, but fearlessly opened up to find Tony and Freddie standing there. He knew Tony immediately, but his mouth fell open, surprised to see him. The young black guy was wearing a good quality gray chauffeur's uniform and cap, therefore needing no explanation.

"Hallo, Barry. Pete asked me to bring something for you. This 'ere's Freddie. Can we come in? Take your cap off, lad."

"Hiya Freddie, come on in, here into the sitting room. My God, Tony, how come you look just the same? Easy life is it, taking care of the superstar?"

Tony grinned and shrugged off the question, knowing Barry was overcome with awkwardness, turning around in circles as he led them into the house, stopping at the bottom of the stairs to call for Carol. He grinned over his shoulder at Tony as he gestured with his eyes up there, and down to his half-dressed condition. A cocky boys' exchange about what they'd been interrupted doing in the middle of the afternoon

"Carol! We got company. 'ow about some tea?"

"Go put the kettle on, Freddie," said Tony. "He's good in the kitchen, right through there is it?"

Barry took Freddie's cap and Tony's coat and scarf, grinning foolishly.

"Some things never change, mate," said Tony, embracing the question and everything around him with a chuckle. He went directly to the big sofa in the living room, sat down and reached in his pocket for a folded envelope, handing it up to Barry.

"There's two checks in there. Don't put them both in at once. He doesn't want your bank asking you tax questions, you know. Save the second one for at least a month."

"Yeah, bet our Pete knows all the tax dodges." Barry couldn't resist taking a peek inside the envelope, after tearing at it roughly, and his eyes lit up.

"Two fives? I can't believe it, he said five."

"Don't be overwhelmed, Barry. He's very aware you don't get royalties from the old material, as he wrote everything, though it's not huge, mind you, pays the housekeeping."

Barry's eyes were shining as he studied the checks. Then he poked around inside the envelope.

"No note?"

"What, Pete put anything in writing?"

"Yeah, right. Silly me. Thanks anyway, mate. And thanks for coming all the way up here with it. I don't get it. Doesn't he trust 'er Majesty's mail either?"

"No, it wasn't just that, Barry. Something I want to discuss with you. Don't worry about Freddie. Knows everything, and cares about none of it. Anyway the boss got him to sign a disclaimer so he's not much use to the tabloids and he gets a nice salary."

"I can hear him in the kitchen talking to Carol."

"He's a good lad, doesn't drink, but he loves to eat. Cake, cookies…"

"Plenty of that here."

"Thought so. You've got that look. Never mind, I'll get straight to the point. Understand you know all there is to know about this whacko Mr. X character. I need some background, want to locate him."

Barry sat down beside Tony with a thump, and an amazed look.

"I can't believe this. Locate him? You? What for? It's what I've been thinking ever since Pete told me. It's driving me mad, Carol too, she's 'ad it with me, going on about King Leo, like she said I'm making some kind of god of him. No-one understands. I can't let him get away with it, what he did to me, to us I mean."

"Slow down, man." Tony reached over and gently shook Barry by one shoulder, looking him deep in the eyes.

"Why don't you start by giving me the Acid King's real name?"

"It's Leonard Rivkin."

"Don't get worked up, she's right, it's not worth it. This is just business. Pete hasn't said a word. This is my decision, not his. I don't like to have untidy stuff around the place. That's what he is, Mister Rivkin. Litter."

The two middle aged men sat squashed up together on a worn sofa, sharing a moment of manic insanity, too far out of reach for normal people. They understood each other, it was briefly comforting. Barry broke the spell by bouncing to his feet and rubbing damp palms on his jeans.

"Don't move, I've got everything on the man, it's all in the scrapbooks. I'll be right back. Ah, tea! Carol, this is my old friend Tony Winston, one of the original group. Now he's Pete's er....?"

"Right hand man. That's what Pete likes to call me."

Tony rose to his feet as he said this and took the heavy loaded tray out of Carol's hands, looking at her full in the eyes with a very warm smile. Carol returned his smile with a new glow.

CHAPTER 19

Pete's House – Tony's Bedroom

It was almost 1 a.m., when Tony got home, after dropping off Freddie in Fulham, a perfect time to make that transatlantic call. Thanks to his network of music biz buddies he knew exactly where to find the Swindon Lodge tour itinerary and reach Reggie Banfield, a long-time friend who could provide him with some information. He used his private line.

CHAPTER 20

Jacksonville, Florida

In a typically bland chain hotel room for Swindon Lodge's continuing big band tour, Reggie picked up the ringing phone, still dozing off in front of the television, and answered it with authority from force of habit.

"Banfield here."

"Reggie! Tony Winston."

" 'allo darlin'. What's up?"

"Not much. You know, life in the country manor with the squire. What about you? Rough is it? On the road with his Lordship?"

"Not bad this time. Bet yours is just the same on tour."

"Yes mate, worse in fact. Which is why he never does it any more, seeing as there's no one left to take the aggro, now he doesn't actually have a band. Best for all of us he prefers staying at home putting it together technically. He likes producing, it gives him lots of time to tinker."

"It's all about control, I think. What can I do for you?"

"We're looking for someone in Los Angeles, I need a private eye type who can help track him down. I was thinking of that security guy everyone uses, built like a shit house door, used to be a football player, you know the one."

"Yeah, I know. That's gotta be Vince Axle. Smashed ankle took him out of the game. You're right, his company's into all areas of security. I'll give you his number. What's he done, then, the perpetrator? Apart from making a big mistake if he's pissed off your angry little geezer."

"Oh, money of course…unpaid royalties, that kind of stuff. He can't help himself, Pete, being vengeful with an elephant's memory. It comes from all the wasted years. Anyway I got the guy's real name, but he hasn't used it for ages apparently. So we need to dig around to trace his current name. Sounds like Vince Axle is my man."

"Give us a second, I'll get my book."

***

Tony didn't waste a stroke, sizing up the two numbers on his pad, noting from his slim expensive watch that the security company office wouldn't be open. He'd try home first. He got lucky, Vince answered right away. Tony introduced himself, briefly described what he wanted, and his ears heard just the right answers. Vince was too young at thirty-seven to have any ties to the rock and roll legends he served so well, but he was suitably deferential and knew most of the names.

"I'll do my best to find the missing person, but if you say his last contact was Madeleine Raleigh when she was on a recent trip to L.A., then I was her last contact. She came to see Swindon Lodge at the Rose Bowl, few nights ago. I was on the VIP gate."

"Was she with anyone?"

"Madeleine Raleigh? No, she arrived alone. But she left with two people, who must have been on the management's list if she met them in there. Want me to check that for you?"

"Not to worry, I can ask Reggie, he's where I got your number. I've got the itinerary here."

"Yeah, they've got two more gigs in Florida. Okay then, tomorrow morning I'll try for a security check on this name, even if he hasn't used it for years. Worth the shot. They'll run it through all kinds of records. Could take a while. I'll get right on it first thing tomorrow."

"Good. Just call me when you get something. No, better idea, call Reggie, I'll give you his cell number, I want to keep it between ourselves for now."

"You want me to follow up on any of this?"

"Not until we talk. Thanks. And give me some idea of your rates now, and your address so I can send you an advance, I can wire it to your bank if you like."

CHAPTER 21

The M1 – Heading South - Monday

Carol gripped the steering wheel with patient determination, the qualities a nurse inherited from her job, and in her particular case, minding the turbulent life of Barry Turnbull, slumped asleep in the seat beside her, snoring lightly. The little Ford Prefect kept its own consistent pace, battling along in the slow lane, well behind the capabilities of all the cars that swooped by them, but as intent as its passengers on getting there in the end.

Barry opened his eyes but stayed in a slouched position, gazing moodily into the distance. Carol noticed he was awake.

"You're still convinced, Barry, this is a wise thing to do?"

"No, not wise, but I just gotta, that's all. Unfinished business. It can get on your tit if you let it, and you know what?"

She waited for him to continue his train of thought.

"I'm getting too old to be carrying this thing much longer."

"Yeah, you are getting on a bit."

"Enough of your bloody mouth, Miss know it all. Just keep driving."

"I won't, if you start annoying me. I'll just drive into the first food stop and leave you there, miserable bugger...."

"Hey, I fancy some chips. That's a good idea. When's the next one?" He leaned over and squeezed her knee suggestively, making her squeak. You know I don't mean any of it, love. I just take it out on you."

"You can say that again. Here we go. Five miles to the next rest stop."

***

Nicely stuffed with a hefty portion of halibut and chips washed down with three cups of strong sweet tea, Barry dozed off again, in spite of a blurring montage of press clippings and familiar images frozen in time. Pete and Barry leaving court after the sentencing, theatrical bravado forcing Pete to wave his manacled hands at the crowd, laughing while Barry kept his eyes down, away from the adoring fans, ashamed and terrified.

Sleep wafted Barry into an actual memory for the first time in all those years, not the images but how it felt to be there when he realized that doom had struck and incarceration was the verdict, his stomach threatening to rip apart with pain. How long the dream lasted he didn't know, probably just seconds, but the horror came up from inside and sucked him into an abyss of black despair. He wanted to wake up but he couldn't. He struggled against it but something kept him there, forcing him to remember.

Barry flailed his arms and moaned in a way that brought Carol out of her own thoughts in a second. She reached out and gripped Barry's arm and spoke very sharply.

"Barry. It's alright. It's alright. I'm here. Wake up. Come on Barry."

She saw that tears were running down his face and she felt the agony for him. Barry took the clean tissue she passed him and nodded.

"S'okay, Carol. I'm okay. I just went back there, Carol. It was so vivid, that's never happened before. I can handle it, honestly."

"Did you take your valium?"

"No."

"Well, take it. Right now. And don't do that to me for Christ's sake, Barry. There's some water. Get it down. And pull yourself together. In twenty-five minutes we'll be there. What do you think of this countryside?"

"It's beautiful. Makes me really hate him."

"Well, that's helpful. We've got to go through with this thing now, I'm dreading it, quite honestly, I'm just doing it for you. I still wish you'd called ahead."

"No! I can read him too well. Didn't want him to know we're coming."

"Can you imagine what it's like for me? I'm sure that Chinese girlfriend is a cold fish, and he will be totally grand, you know it. He'll treat us like the poor relations."

"That's what we are, darlin', it's all attitude. Make out like you don't give a fuck."

CHAPTER 22

Pete's House, Virginia Water

In the kitchen Tony was hunched over the dining table, working on accounts, while his mother polished the top of the oven. The peaceful atmosphere was broken by a very loud series of buzzes.

"Hey, Mum, someone at the gate. Want to get it for me? Just adding up here."

Outside the defensive wrought iron gates of the Stebbings estate, the Ford Prefect parked nearby with the engine running, and Carol gripping the steering wheel. Barry leaned into the intercom punching numbers at random. When the crackle of static and the kindly woman's voice came through, Barry announced himself, barely controlling the nerves in his voice.

"This is bloody embarrassing," Carol hissed as the gate slowly opened and Barry leapt into the car as if there were no time to catch it before it closed again.

CHAPTER 23

Pete's Recording Studio

"Look, don't go on about it, Barry. We can cope."

Pete paced around the room while Barry slouched resentfully in a seasoned leather Chesterfield armchair, feeling as small as he looked in it, and noting the aristocratic surroundings and Pete's impeccable casual clothes.

"We've got tons of room here. Carol's getting on fine with Tony's mother, they're messing about in the kitchen just like old pals. You can stay for a few days, just don't look at me like you want me to feel fucking guilt for being successful, it's pissing me off."

Barry shot him a withering look.

"How about a beer, then?" Pete offered.

"Oh, all this, and you're still drinking beer?"

"Would you rather have champagne?"

"No, fer crying out loud. A beer's fine. Don't you have to ring for the staff? You know, pull one of them ropes by the fireplace?"

"You're a sarcastic bastard, Barry. I have a bar fridge in here. Heineken okay?"

"I'll take it. No glass."

"You're not getting one. I'm going to play you some tracks now, whether you like it or not. It's what I'm working on currently, and you can get belligerent about it after, I don't care, just bloody listen."

They both tipped their bottles back and savored the cold beer. A hint of a smile touched Barry's mouth as he wiped it.

"Sorry, man, I'm just going through giant therapy stuff right now. The past came up and hit me in the face, and I'm kind of wallowing in it. Thinking about you and how our lives went in different directions. Weird, isn't it?"

"We dealt with it in different ways, I did my crack-up in Jamaica. Ganja, sex and reggae got me through it. It was a nightmare hearing about you going over the top like that but I couldn't have helped you for one second. Couldn't even help Madeleine, she went off the deep end worse than both of us, then marrying that creep."

"I understand that creep saved her life and turned it around."

"Did you ever hear she had our daughter and didn't tell me for years?"

"Yeah, quite recently I did. That struck me as being really weird."

"She did it for me, said I couldn't have coped, she was right about that. And it's why she married little lord whatsit, so I thought the baby was his, pity he didn't last long. Then she went off the rails again, and her mum took over. Charlotte's a fantastic girl, wait till you meet her. She's got more natural survivor's guts than us all."

Barry drained the bottle, lost in thought again.

"Ready for another? You know, face it Barry, we're all miraculous survivors. Kids today would take the whole thing with more ease than we did. We were naïve about the power of the law, and pretty arrogant to think they wouldn't try to wipe us out for being a public nuisance. We flaunted it, mate. We asked for it."

"So why can't we get over it?"

Pete's eyes turned into slits at Barry's question. But he said nothing, just turned his back and went over to the tape machines, flicking a switch to fill the room with of music. Straight off there was a rich, rhythmic roundness to the melody and Barry looked up in surprise. He hadn't expected to like it so much and so soon.

After a few compelling bars of buildup, Pete's voice came on, and it was magnificent. He moved around the room to the rhythm, not showing off yet, glancing often at Barry's face to catch his reaction, liking what he saw. Barry's music habit got to him, his body took up the beat and he grinned as Pete caught his eye this time and grinned back. The years fell away and they were kids in a band again.

Two tracks later Pete switched off the music and sat down.

"There's more like that. What do you think? Don't hold back."

"They're good. You're great. You know that. Want the truth? You've made it. It's the best music you've ever made and I'm fucking jealous not to be involved with it. But you know, it also pisses me off because I was better'n you back then, that was my problem, just being on the same stage as you. I had a bigger voice and you had a prettier act. I look at the old promos and what I see is you crowding me out, wagging your ass and making me look like a stiff."

"I didn't know you hated me, dear."

"That's stupid. I didn't hate you, not now nor then. Just under your spell like everyone else. You took over, it went with your personality, lead singer, director, lording it, and I withdrew from the competition."

"That's why you started hiding behind those old native drums, eh, Barry?"

"Yeah that's exactly how you managed to belittle me, snide bugger. I need another beer."

Barry got up clumsily and lurched over to the bar, trying to open the fridge. Pete came over and moved him aside.

"I'll do that. This is my house."

"Don't shove me. And you don't have to remind if it's your bloody mansion, you bloody snob."

To emphasize this remark, Barry pushed Pete away with a heavy hand on his shoulder, and Pete pushed back. It suddenly got worse and escalated into a real scuffle, with both men almost losing their footing as the punches were thrown. They were now fighting in an ugly unprofessional style, both puffing and gasping, until Barry backed onto the chair, lost his balance and slid to the ground, kicking away a small table so the lamp and other items on it crashed on the parquet floor. Pete backed away and stood there, heaving for breath and quite shocked at what had happened.

Carol and Tony rushed into the room and assessed the scene. Carol's first thought was to attend to Barry and check out his condition. She felt his pulse and wiped his brow, but she felt compelled to apologize for him too.

"I'm so sorry, Pete. I should have known he was building up to a fight. He's been in his comfy cocoon up north all these years, and seeing how you live got him worked up. He's not really nasty at heart."

"S'alright, Carol. I know him well enough too. He's certainly not in condition for brawling but I'm glad he's still got the cocky attitude. It's good. You know it's good for both of us. What do you think, Turnbull, feeling better?"

"You can bring that champagne on now, Sport," said Barry with a grin.

Pete quickly checked out the look on Carol's face, and nodded at her.

"It's okay folks. You can go back to the bridge game. The boys still have a bit to catch up with. He's right as rain, Carol, don't worry about him."

CHAPTER 24

FBI Headquarters, Manhattan

Monday

During most of the years FBI Agent Cortez had slaved the small stuff in the bureau, hoping there'd be some news about Leonard Rivkin, he wondered if he had quietly given up but not admitted it to himself. It wasn't hope, it was habit. Now the note was in front of him, undeniably black and white, he had a chilled ghostly feeling that both hope and denial were over.

The dead had stirred. Someone had gone into the Rivkin file.

The note was written casually by a computer clerk who had no idea of the jolt she was delivering, and he moved around on the office computer screen until he stepped into the basement in which he'd placed the bait. He felt the glow of triumph as he realized that his guess was on target. That sooner or later, with the growing availability of computer database, and renewed curiosity about the sixties, some person from somewhere would be looking for this name. Now he had to confront it, he didn't know what to do.

Someone else needed the computer, standing over him snapping a sheaf of paperwork with urgency and irritation, so he decided to take an early lunch break, get away from the usual

Monday morning pressure, go home and study his private notes on the case.

***

Over a microwaved something that he didn't bother to take out of the container, Cortez flipped with his free hand through the reference books he'd collected on the subject of Leonard Rivkin, his own personal Houdini. He needed a refresher course, not in the desire for justice that would never go away, but in the logistics and other details. He wasn't hiding official papers, but some of these were over ten years old, and would have been assigned to the basement files, and hard to reach, so he had made duplicates where necessary. The ADIC didn't have to know.

He decided to trace the source of the enquiry at the office at the end of the day when most of the agents had gone, and take it from there. He had no idea who it could be and he pondered the possibilities. Some sixties nostalgia buff writing a story, a serious journalist maybe, a family member? He started to shake with anticipation, looking forward to a few hours to himself on the computer.

***

Cortez was walking towards his desk when he saw the big girl waving at him. He looked at her enquiringly without changing course.

"Hey, Cortez, you got another break-in on that code number. Just after you went to lunch," she chirped.

He stopped on a dime then managed to wave back and casually nod his okay.

This was uncanny. Seven years of nothing, now two enquiries in a day. He rushed to his desk, glanced at the details on her note, then sat down at the big computer and turned it on. He couldn't wait for privacy. Not for the first time Cortez marveled at the power of the bureau's technology as it quickly revealed that the first enquiry had come from a Los Angeles based security group.

He wasn't quite sure what kind of business this implied, so he tracked down the company profile, which revealed an organization with offices in New York, Miami and Los Angeles that provided guards to the entertainment business among other things. It was a top level service, ranging from personal bodyguards for big name celebrities in movies and music, long term or one night only, down to club bouncers and full units of security men to control special events, including sports and stadium concerts. The company also checked background references for security purposes for their clients. They even did private eye work for the right people. He got the impression that it was a cover for some heavy duty clients, something like Kroll.

Cortez started to tingle. He could see a connection. Either Rivkin was a prospective employee whose background was being checked, or someone else was looking for him. This was a hot trail. He decided to set up a contact with the security company pronto because he sensed he could get away with this without revealing his hand.

Now he watched the invisible wheels of the FBI surveillance machine turning out the identity of the second enquiry. He'd expected it to be the original enquirer, with a follow up, but he squirmed in his chair from the bolt of electric shock when he saw the name of a Los Angeles newspaper. What was going on? Did this mean that his fugitive was in that city?

Cortez was already packing a bag in his head as he nosed further into the source of the enquiry. It actually came from a local independent weekly publication, using the computer system of a big media syndicate out West that owned both papers. And there was a source. A staff investigative journalist, name of Ann Stapleton.

Cortez let go of his breath, hadn't realized he'd been holding it this long. He was staggered by these two great strikes of fortune. Action at last.

He did some more checking in this challenging system to look further into the paper, not expecting much, but there was all the information right in his face, meaning the FBI had tabs on this journal. Cortez wasn't surprised when he read more of the interesting details. The paper was one of those recent trendy vehicles for alternative areas of the city's lifestyle, like the old New York Village Voice, from underground theater to controversial local and seemingly anti-right wing national politics. The writer herself contributed a regular column on new music, the club scene and independent movies.

Cortez indulged himself in guessing that she might be writing some sixties flashback piece which featured The Veils and their drug bust, and needed to know more about the dealer on the scene. It was likely she didn't know who he was or where he was either. But why this story now, and what was the connection to the security investigator? That last word lit a bright bulb in his head. It couldn't be just a coincidence. He had to jump in before some other jackal sniffed out his prey.

His mind was racing. Here he was, a veteran agent losing his common sense from excitement. He hadn't felt emotions like this for years.

He calmed himself down and came to a quick conclusion. No way could he do this officially, and he had to do it alone. Cortez had taken such a lone ranger position on this long forgotten manhunt he wouldn't know how to requisition for the trip. Besides, vengeance wasn't in the Bureau's official conduct rules, and it was only a long shot.

He had some uncollected sick days and a long weekend coming up. He quickly got to work organizing his trip to L.A., drew up a list of items to take care of. On a piece of paper with a pen. This was for his eyes only. Once he'd ticked off most of the items he dialed the number in L.A. on a direct line so the security company couldn't trace it. Cortez wanted his visit to be very casual. A special plane trip from the east coast would tip anyone off. Paranoia was a justified job requirement here.

The next move was easy. The enquiry came from a V. Axle and in a moment Vince was on the line, happy to hear a response so quickly, and volunteering information without any questions from Cortez, who stood up and started pacing as Vince explained that a company client wanted to trace Leonard Rivkin who was now using a different name. The client had no address or other I.D., just a rough description: age, height, color of eyes. It had been some years since the previous contact. Something to do with unfinished business. The man had recently been seen in Los Angeles, during this current week in fact, but there was no way to trace his location without some help.

***

So he was still alive. Cortez recognized this amazing fact with a series of physical reactions. To his surprise he found he was shaking again and his suddenly weak legs forced him to sit down. He wiped sweat off his forehead with the back of his other hand as he politely continued the conversation with Vince, setting a time to visit his office the day after tomorrow.

Yes, he lied, Mr. Leonard Rivkin had been an employee of his organization and he was happy to help Vince's client locate a former business associate, but it would have to be confidential, hence a personal meeting was more appropriate. He was sorry not be able to schedule something today but important meetings with out of state clients at his downtown office made that impossible. However, tomorrow around mid-day perhaps, he would call and confirm that early in the morning. He was shocked at himself, this reasonable professional, that he had so suddenly decided to catch a plane tonight, whatever it took.

Cortez smiled to himself when he thought of the reaction he would get from Vince seeing a handsome well-dressed black man waiting in the company lobby. Cortez always enjoyed this one.

He had to play a stealth game with this new connection, helping to find the man he was actually seeking himself. Cortez wanted to collect all the input first, including Ann Stapleton and a hunch she might be more clued in on Rivkin than this guy. Who had seen him and where? How did the client get to hear about it so fast?

Cortez remained calm and efficient after putting down the phone, but he wanted to scream out in rage because Leonard Rivkin was still alive after killing a government agent, his mentor and closest friend in the Bureau. He'd never forgotten what it was like to see Norman lying down there, white and cold, his skull crushed with what the autopsy showed to be one brutal blow with his own baseball bat.

Rivkin had guaranteed both his insurance and vulnerability by taking off with his own file. What was inside it no government agency would want to share with the public.

Cortez had sat for over an hour with his friend's body, killed and abandoned in the safe house by a man he'd done so much to help. Protecting him from his previous masters who considered him disposable. Any exposure could be deadly, and Rivkin knew that.

There was never any sign of him during the long time Cortez spent looking, years of endless phone calls, useless leads, boring checks of voting records, drivers licenses, social security, state by state. It was a solid wall of nothing.

What finally came to Cortez was the acceptance that Rivkin had created his very own witness protection identity and escaped into it. Probably got a fake passport and left the country. It was no solace. And it didn't mean he gave up hope, but at least he began to contemplate the relief of sleeping all the way through a night.

Now, Cortez sharply reminded himself, snapping out of those shadows, it was time to put on the mask that would serve him for the next ten days. Settle the score. Move swiftly, decisively, leave no tracks and return to his desk a satisfied man.

Cortez tried to slip quietly away for his vacation, but the now too helpful file worker hailed him loudly on the way out.

"Hey, have a good time, Cortez. I thought it was hot and humid as hell in Key West Florida this time of year."

"Hey, I'm working on my tan."

CHAPTER 25

Pete's House, Virginia Water

The two aging rockers had drunk their way through most of a magnum of very good champagne and into a nice rosy mood, feeling much better after their fight. They had experienced a stimulating workout, of adrenalin and emotions, and made a bridge between their apartheid lives.

"Yer know, I had to say that about singing better than you, Pete, didn't I? It was choking me, because it's bloody true and you know it is. You were way ahead of me in your vision of where the band was going, that was your gift, Pete. I was the big voice but you were a marketing genius before anyone knew about it."

"Don't forget Colonel Parker."

"Oh, I beg his fucking pardon. And modesty doesn't suit you, darlin'. You knew enough to get rid of Mark before anyone noticed he was there, pounding the keyboards with his pudgy fingers, great in pubs, but you knew where The Veils could go. Not to mention old Tony, with his fifties beat thing. I would have been next, no doubt. If we 'adn't landed in the nick."

"Don't feel sorry for Mark. A happy polar opposite, he sends me a card every Christmas with a family portrait. Manager of the bank, big pay, pension, set for life."

"Death, you mean."

"Yeah, well, you could say that. And as for Tony, well, look at him, lord of the manor. But you're exactly right. We never resolved the issue.

We were just kids though, flapping our egos around. Is that what it's about, your turning up like this?"

"It's connected, I suppose. It's always been about the competition, rubs off on everything. I remember you always got the girls I'd noticed first, wham you just worked the moves faster. You wiggled your ass and stunned them with your intellect."

"I think time has affected your imagination. I don't remember any of that."

"Actually I was getting worked up because I'm convinced you know where Leonard Rivkin is and you won't tell me because you know what I'd do to him."

"Well, I don't. Didn't ask. Don't care."

"Don't tell me that, Pete, I don't believe you. You, not curious? Don't blag me. You're dying to know where he is, what he's been doing all these years, who he really was, why he snitched on us? Admit it."

"Barry, you gotta understand. I cannot allow myself to be thrown into chaos by the reappearance of a ghost. I just can't."

"Denial, thy name is Pete Stebbings."

"And neither should you, you owe it to Carol. Christ man, you'd be dead or in a straitjacket and you're gonna put her back through that again? If you do, you're a raving selfish bastard."

"Alright, back off. You made a good point."

They fell into a silence while Pete poured more chilled champagne. Barry slurped his noisily, not aware of the judgmental flicks Pete's eyes were throwing him. The silence was not uncomfortable, benign acceptance across the great divide, a calm brought on by time. They'd started as brothers, it seemed possible after the long journey they could end up the same.

Tony, consummate butler, had probably registered the silence from very close to the keyhole, his entrance was so perfectly timed.

"Food's on the table, gentlemen."

Barry was on his feet surprisingly fast. His body responded to the key word in a similar way to his fellow pharmaceutical travelers, the lab rats. He knew where the kitchen was and disappeared in that direction. Pete and Tony lingered behind, Pete filling his glass one more time. Tony made an *er* sound to indicate he wanted to speak, and Pete listened.

"You alright with them staying a couple of nights then?"

"Course. It's pathetic to think of sending them back up the M1 in that thing. I saw it out there. Anything you can do with it, Tony? One of your local mechanics could maybe fix a few things, like an oil change? Don't let 'em get carried away."

"I'll take care of it, guv. Nice thinking."

Pete grunted as if to wave away the compliment, out of character as it was. He led the way to his dining room. Tony following up with the champagne bucket and Barry's glass.

***

Carol looked around the table and agreed with herself that this was one of the best evenings she'd ever had. Tony and his mum had made her feel part of the domestic family, Ling Pai had not stopped smiling and already given her a package of aromatherapy aids for bath and bed, including a lavender filled little pillow for her eyes, which she was supposed to keep in the freezer.

Along with that she'd watched a gourmet three-course meal being prepared and been given taste treats of everything, plus several glasses of champagne, then the delicious dinner itself. The best part was seeing Barry unraveled from his usual uptight anger on a short fuse, loose-limbed and chipper.

"Well, I don't know what you two talked about in there," she ventured boldly. "But you certainly came out in a good mood."

"We cleared the air, my darling wife. We went through decades of history and arrived at the present. By way of Mister X, of course. And we've both admitted we're over that, and don't want to hear his name again."

Nobody noticed that two people didn't look up from their plates.

Pete lifted his glass to confirm this fact, like a toast.

"To Old King Leo, for the last time. We have to respect him in his role of catalyst, he played a fateful role in our lives, and now he is again. Chances are he's suffered more than we did. At least we don't have to hide from anyone. Poor bastard, what kind of life has he had? Lonely, I bet. And look at us, it's like old times. Right, Barry?"

"Here's to it, man," said Barry, clinking glasses with Pete.

Here's to what, was the question in his eyes.

CHAPTER 26

Wrightman Security Inc., Wilshire Boulevard, Los Angeles - Tuesday

Cortez rose to greet the young security guard when he walked into the lobby to find his guest, easing the obvious reaction he expected from Vince Axle with a warm firm shake and his winning smile. As an experienced FBI agent he could discern the impact, although it appeared on the younger man's face for a second only. It was on such tiny revelations that Cortez gained his success over the years. He loved the challenge of gaining someone's confidence without having to hold up the famous badge. His one and only Armani suit and the accessories that went with it were what counted here in L.A., and in a company that rated their clients by money and style.

This is going to be fun, he thought as Vince awkwardly ushered him into a small conference room, not his office, indicating that his employee ranking was on the level of small open cubicle. That was a useful detail to make use of somehow.

"Where do we start?" Cortez asked cheerfully. "Actually, I'll answer my own question. Let me introduce myself again. Here's my card. My business has something in common with yours. Security. Believe me it will be the buzzword of this century. Ours is the very confidential recovery of missing persons, somewhere between collection agency and bail bondsman, with government connections of a sort. We seem to be looking for the same person."

"Well, that's convenient." Vince glanced at the card. "But you said he was employed by your company."

"He was on our payroll, yes. After that time he lost contact and we've recently found a need for his services. For reasons I can't divulge. You could call it sources and methods."

"Sounds important."

"Our problem, Vince, is that neither of us know his current identity. It's possible he will be using one of several. I'm hoping you can give me a person to connect him with. That will be enough for me to track him down."

He looked hopefully at Vince but there was no response.

"Which I must do, I hope you understand, with utmost care and discretion because of client confidentiality. Hate to use that word, but he has the potential to disappear easily."

"Understood. I've got confidentiality here, too. My client doesn't want his name to be revealed."

"If there's a contact you can supply me with then I will most certainly give you all the information I get. There's no reason not to, and you will be able to satisfy your client's needs. And get paid for it, I hope."

Vince grinned. "No problem there. What I do know is that a trusted friend of my client saw Rivkin recently in a late night club in L.A."

"Who?"

"Madeleine Raleigh. She was a star of some kind back in the sixties, everyone knew her. Here's the coincidence. She turned up at the Rose

Bowl for the Swindon Lodge show last week. I was on the VIP. security gate."

"Who was she with?"

"She was alone, and I never saw her again. So that's a dead end. I don't know the name of the club either."

"Is there a time factor in your delivering the man's current identity and whereabouts to your client?"

"No."

"Excellent. Then we have an understanding. That 800 number on my card gets my answering service. Feel free to leave a message if you like. I'm always on the move. Be assured I will call you as soon as I get a lead."

They parted like compatriots. This was perfect. Cortez knew he was way ahead of Vince Axle. Next stop Miss Stapleton. It only took a twitch of the brain cells for him to imagine a connection between this Madeleine and the sixties story the other woman was researching. Rivkin's embarrassing escapade in England. That was it. He thought her name was familiar. It was falling into place. This was going to be easy.

CHAPTER 27

Pete's House

The atmosphere during the morning following their dramatic reunion dinner was convivial and a great relief to everyone in the household. Tony's mum, who knew nothing of the details but was accustomed to being in the eye of the storm without asking any questions, exercised her authority role in the family by making fresh croissants for breakfast and watching the ecstatic, *ooohs* and *aaahs* as people slapped on the butter and homemade apricot jam and gobbled up every one of them.

Neither Barry nor Carol really wanted to leave, and allowed themselves to be persuaded that before they drove back up north they should walk down to the local public house for a late lunch and a few glasses of ale. Barry relished being in the company of superstar Pete, especially in the pub, where he was recognized immediately and patted on the back more than a prize cow. Pete was gracious and amicable. Ling Pai didn't join them at the pub, nor Mum.

But Carol and Tony were in full conversation, ambling along together like old friends while Tony told her that he intended to keep up the good connection, and he would be calling her, quipping to Barry that he was not to be jealous. Pete jested by adding that Barry had nothing to fear from Tony, who was married to his mum and her home cooking anyway.

There was no talk of Mister X and none of them knew that the fast car whose motor they had revved up was now being driven by someone else on the other side of the Atlantic.

CHAPTER 28

Outside Ann's Apartment – Tuesday

Cortez decided it wasn't such a bad day for the first one of tracking Ann Stapleton, he couldn't expect a bull's-eye too soon, and he was learning something about the environs of Los Angeles, at least those chosen by this particular lady. He'd started off early in the afternoon at the office of the *Weekly Independent*, charmed the receptionist with a two-step about an appointment he thought he had, finding out that Ann Stapleton was not a regular office worker but was definitely on her way in during the next hour. He'd watched her arrive from a doorway across the road, but she was out again so fast he almost had a heart attack getting back to his carefully parked car before she drove out of his sight.

The rest of the day was spent following her discreetly to a health food store, three book shops, a lending library, dry cleaners, then a couple of hours waiting outside a small movie production office off Melrose, before she finally led him to her home in what he now knew was West Hollywood. It was a sigh of relief that at least he now knew where she lived, and could use that as a base from which to wait patiently and hopefully for her to lead him to Leonard Rivkin.

That seven o'clock turned out to be the end of her day was something of a disappointment, and waiting another five hours to be sure of that fact was tedious, but the stakes were high and he filled his thoughts with optimism.

He'd selected a small hotel in the area for price and convenience, but when it came to finding a place for dinner he was disappointed again to find one that didn't have a crowded gay clientele. It wasn't the gay part, that never bothered him; it was that zest and noisy chatter. It didn't suit his mood, so he ended up in an even noisier place on the corner next to the Troubadour which reminded him of New York.

CHAPTER 29

Long Beach Auditorium

Vince Axle didn't smile much on the job. He considered it a professional obligation that his size and presence be a serious threat to troublemakers, whether they were sports fans or music hysterics. He'd noticed lately that potential mayhem seemed to thrive amongst the teen rock fans. As well as keeping his keen eyes roving around the crowds, watching for violent movements, he kept himself busy thinking a lot. Inside he laughed at the ideas he came up with, this solitary gladiator, and how surprised most people would be at the intelligence he possessed, behind the grim face atop the massive body.

He'd spent most of the night thinking hard about the visit from Cortez, working out what was phony about the man and why. He knew he should try to check him out on the office computer, but he hadn't yet. The machine intimidated him for one thing. He'd managed to follow very confusing instructions for the $500 he was getting from the man Reggie. Vince was more interested in direct contact, with the visual aides to guide him, and his gut instinct, which never failed.

On a gut level he looked at the facts. A handsome, well-groomed middle-aged black dude in an expensive suit turns up out of nowhere in response to an enquiry he's registered for a man's name. A surprisingly immediate response. That was a mystery in itself. He tells Vince nothing, but is more interested in finding out the man's whereabouts himself. That's provocative. He hands over a business card that could have been printed this morning. He casually mentions 'government connections'. That really tweaked the curiosity.

Vince was pleased with himself for being quick to withhold one vital piece of information: the people Madeleine Raleigh left with. He saw them, and knew she must have met them in the green room, so they would be on Swindon Lodge's backstage pass list. What really rankled him was the superiority that the black man conveyed. Treating him like a dork. Therefore I'll behave like one, Vince decided during Prince's hopefully last encore song.

CHAPTER 30

Pete's House, Virginia Water - Wednesday

Pete, Tony and Ling Pai arrived at the outside gate, now slowly opening to admit them after an early morning run. Tony was doing most of the panting, Pete was still in good form though his face registered relief to be back, and Ling Pai looked ready to do it all over again. She sprinted ahead, calling over her shoulder.

"Yoga in ten minutes, Pete."

"Okay dear," said Pete, rolling his eyes at Tony, with a resigned half smile.

"Can I have a word Pete? Before you go in."

Pete put his hands on his hips, bent over, took some huge breaths in and out, and nodded.

"Something interesting I heard. Vis-à-vis Madeleine's call the other day. Just chewing the fat over the phone with one of my management friends in the States, Reggie actually. On my private line."

"What then?"

"She met that Mister X through an old friend of hers. She didn't just run into him in a club."

"Really now? Who was it? Anyone we know?"

"Yes, actually. None other than Ann Mayberry, she's Ann Stapleton now. I barely remember her, but you would. She was the girlfriend of Tarquin...."

"Blimey, of course I do. A very serious little dolly bird she was. Never saw her since the funeral, she vanished. This is a mindblower you came up with, Tony."

"Yeah, she works at something called *The Weekly Independent*."

"Great. Well, keep me up to date on anything else you find out. Only out of curiosity, mind. I've left that whole era behind."

"Right you are, guv."

***

Pete and Ling Pai lay on their yoga mats in the final prone position after an intense hour of stretching and breathing. The music had come to an end. Tony, on the other side of the door, had timed their regular session and knew it was safe to give a knock and walk in, clearing his throat politely, another ritual.

"Just another thing, Pete. I'm scheduling the Bentley for an oil change and tune up for the next two days. Anything you need it for that's not on my calendar?"

"No, mate. Matter of fact I'm going to Los Angeles, just made up my mind lying here. Got to talk to those two record companies, and might as well see the persistent film geezer, you know the one. So about three days. Wouldn't mind leaving tomorrow, back Monday. Put me in that new trendy place on Sunset. It's in the current *Vanity Fair*. Splash out with the room though because it looks a bit boxy, and a view of the pool. Everything else as usual, rental car at the airport. I liked that last one we used, but I don't want any flashy color."

Tony's eyebrows had risen almost into his hairline. Did he hear right? Pete slipping off to L.A.

on his own, and not a word about Mister X? Puzzling. But Tony was patient and knew how to scoop out the truth eventually.

"Right you are. Got it. And I'll make sure your agenda's up to date with phone numbers and addresses there. Any new ones to add?"

"Not that I can think of."

Ling Pai had remained motionless on the floor but some subtle evidence of body tension betrayed her innate sense of insecurity about Pete. Three days removed from her grip and anything could happen to the compulsive alley cat she'd pinned her hopes on. She rose and slipped out of the room before she could be disappointed by Pete's loss of interest.

She was right. Pete's secretive thoughts were currently engaged with the rediscovery of Ann. He was downright curious about her now. After all these years had she become someone he could bond with, he pondered. No one else but God knew this was his private dream. To find his eternal sweetheart, wife and best friend.

He allowed the possibility that years in L.A. after the tragic times in London could have turned her into a hard-nosed phony Brit. He'd met plenty of them in the business over there. Something told him that she would be different. Pete Stebbings, the hopeful romantic, not an image for public consumption, thanks to the bitter rhetoric of many discarded and disqualified women. He always tried to do it without causing pain and anger. He never fucked a girl only once, knowing from early experience what rage the one night stand could evoke in a female. But they still ended up disappointed when he couldn't sustain the lasting relationship most of them craved. He'd have to be subtle with Ann because she'd twig to the fact that he was using her to make contact with Leo, but he was very clear that seeing her again was the stronger mission. He'd have to make sure she would see it the same way. He was starting to feel alive.

He felt a small tremor of guilt from the lingering presence of Ling Pai, the way she just got up and left without a word. How would she react when the inevitable happened? Oh well, don't go there yet, he thought as he turned over on his side preparing to get up and start the day.

The L.A. trip was something to look forward to, he needed a new blood rush. He'd already made up his mind to say yes to the movie. This guy had the energy and originality of Scorsese, everyone wanting to be him over the last ten years of course, but it was only five days of shooting and a ton of cash, plus all the perks, the most important one to Pete being the huge juggernaut of publicity that these Hollywood machines put out.

The media coverage would just embellish everything else he had in the pipeline, and no doubt stir up the two record companies, who were both taking far too much time to commit to a deal. If he made some new headlines they'd be falling over each other to sign him up.

Pete intended to enjoy being brown-nosed by those obsequious Hollywood people who'd been phoning him and flattering him about the role, anticipating with relish the lavish meals and fancy club scenes they'd invite him to before he agreed to accept it. Pete loved not having to pick up the tab. He also liked the screenwriter's clever tongue-in-cheek cameo role as himself surrounded by some eager hot young teens. It was all good. The promise of a lively few days. And he would get to keep the cool outfit. Bottom line he wanted the chance to meet Ann again, and yes he honestly wanted to terminate the obsession with Leo, with no idea what to expect.

***

Tony himself enjoyed the ritual of packing for the trip; he knew exactly what Pete liked to wear in California. He went over to the bookshelf and pulled out a few interesting books, Chuang Tzu, the new one from Hawkings, an old leather bound John Donne and, this took some thinking, a first printing of Simone de Beauvoir's *The Second Sex* in French. Tony chuckled at his last choice. He'd witnessed the awed reaction of American movie people when they saw such literature nonchalantly placed around the suite. When they found out it was actually Pete's current reading material, they were impressed. This one was guaranteed to get Pete laid by a surprised leggy intellectual, a writer perhaps. Tony could picture her quite perfectly. He mentally slapped himself on the wrist for playing with these fantasies. But hadn't it always been this way? *Plus ça change*, as Madame Simone might have said.

CHAPTER 31

Offices of *The Weekly Independent* –Los Angeles

Ann looked at the darkness creeping over the newspaper's main office, then at her watch, and wondered how long she would stay at her desk finishing the story for tomorrow's noon deadline; she couldn't seem to wrap it up. Ann usually worked at home but tonight she had to keep away from the temptation of speaking to Griffin. He had a knack for guessing when she was there, and she hated not being able to pick up her own phone. Having interrupted her concentration on the last three paragraphs, she decided to check with the office answering service, having ignored that chore and the ringing phone for hours now.

The familiar night shift voice greeted her cheerfully with his usual touch of dry humor.

"Good evening, Miss Stapleton. Since you called we've had Mrs. Bennett from the Hollywood Theater at four seventeen, you've got that number? Your friend Janice, she'll call you back, and Mr. Griffin called five times. Do you want the specific times?"

"No, Martin. Just the first and last."

"Four twelve and five minutes ago. The last time he left a message. Said he is deeply concerned because you haven't returned his calls. He made me underline deeply."

Ann just sat there in the pool of light from the desk lamp, and thought very hard about her past relationship with Griffin. It was a see-saw. Up with the joys of feeling alive again when they met, because he had revived her ability to love. Down with the realization that he couldn't reciprocate, more accurately wouldn't reveal himself again after showing her once how much he wanted her. She squirmed with misery, hating herself for succumbing so easily to that one night of fulfillment which he cut off like sudden death. It was a bitter irony that this new insight into his dark torment explained it all. His reasons for not wanting to get close to someone, be intimate, spill the beans, expose his demons.

She tried using this new insight to feel better about her pained ego and frustrated emotions, but nothing got through. Stunned that this man could have held that big a secret, one that played an enormous part in her own life's equally dark horrors, and that for two years she'd had no idea about it. She turned it over and over. It didn't get any easier to accept the rejection. In fact she felt more shocked and duped than before.

Now Ann was thankful not to have met King Leo back then, though Tarquin had apparently spent hours with him. She was unknown to Griffin then, and had a different name now. It meant she didn't have to say a word to him, certainly not yet. Not out of fear, she felt none, although she could imagine his need to eliminate anyone who knew his secret.

Ann laughed, that was too silly. But the dark side was there, the mystery of his friend's murder. She also felt sorry for him. For his years of being a lone wolf, surviving outside the system, using cover names. Did his parents know? They must have, they'd been supplying him with money, or so he said. But he was always vague about his parents, the stories varied, were they alive or not? And where were they? Griffin was cagey about everything personal. Who was Griffin anyway?

Finally she shut down her thoughts and went back to her column, wrapping it with edit and corrections in just over half an hour.

CHAPTER 32

Outside *The Weekly Independent* Offices - Wednesday

Cortez, standing in a doorway across the road from the two-story building which housed the newspaper, was not enjoying himself at all. He'd been here the day before briefly, and he didn't know what to expect as he waited outside her apartment this morning. He had to be ready for the long haul. It was only a hope and a hunch that she would do something that would connect him to Rivkin. So far this woman didn't seem to have any friends.

It took him by surprise when she landed back at the office in the mid-afternoon today, and was still in there, hours later, after all the other staff had left, and hers was the only light burning. He used his powers of deduction to check the date the paper arrived on the street, and match it to a deadline. This was the reason. She was finishing her column. He'd read the last one and got an insight to her lifestyle, and saw her byline photo. Good looking woman. He thought freelance writers would work from home. He wondered why she was working in the office, better typewriters maybe, copiers, yes that made sense.

Cortez sincerely hoped she would be visiting Leonard Rivkin, very soon, and was actually praying for this event when he saw her leave the office building and walk slowly to her car, a ten-year-old Pacer.

It didn't take him long to read the street names and realize that once again this would not be the night, as they made the turns that took her into Holloway Drive and home. He knew enough to linger for another hour or so outside in case she emerged for a late night visit, but the lights eventually went out and he drove back to his West Hollywood hotel. Too tired to give his curiosity an outing in this strange city he knew very little about. The kind of tired that comes from bored rather than frustrated.

CHAPTER 33

Griffin's Place

Griffin was alone for that short period of time before the few close buddies he still had came by for an evening toke, which would be followed by constant arrivals until the clubbers turned up after midnight and stayed through dawn. He was wrapped in nostalgia, rummaging in his shelves for audio tapes, scratched and marked hastily by hand, but he knew exactly what he had and where to locate it. He spent a while playing with images on his editing machine, got impatient, played old music he wrote and sang in the sixties, pacing around restlessly, making phone calls, jabbing at the numbers, leaving terse enigmatic messages, and speaking roughly to someone for a few seconds.

When the phone rang he answered it brusquely, not hiding his ugly mood, saying he was busy writing his new project and to call him later.

Next time the phone rang he snatched it up immediately. It was Ann. As a way of showing the relief he obviously felt, his voice became warm, almost syrupy.

"So, you must have been busy doing something very pressing. You're an important journalist. I should try to remember that."

"Oh, Griffin, you know this publication I work for. Deadlines are a religion. And besides that, I had to dump my piece and write something completely new from scratch. About this controversial movie that's all the rage."

"I haven't seen you for days, and I don't want you to disappear from my life."

Underneath the showy talk his vulnerability was touching, out of character and of course fleeting, she knew.

"Come off it, Griffin. I notice you didn't ask me what controversial movie I've been writing about."

"That's because I know."

"Oh, you do?"

"Yes, it's *I Married My Mom*'"

"Oh. Okay, so you knew. I forgot about your network of gossip slaves."

"I assumed you were spending a lot of time with that nice English friend of yours. The singer, name escapes me...Madeleine of course."

"No, I told you, she went straight back to London next morning, we said our goodbyes that night and she was off."

"And she didn't say anything about the time we met."

"Honestly, Griffin, I don't think you listen to a word I say...."

"Ann, please don't switch moods on me..."

"The last time you asked me that question I told you all she said was that you had told her some private joke or something and she promised not to pass it on. Hell, I didn't even bother to ask her what it was myself. Can't stand jokes anyway."

"Oh, yes, you told me that. I remember now. Well, it's not important anyway. Now what is important is my script here. You did say you were going to give me some guidance with it? I hope you meant it. I need your help."

"The science fiction project?"

"It's a story that reveals the truth about our world. And one day the truth will be seen."

"Well, I was telling you the truth when I said I think it's fascinating and could be very commercial and successful. But..."

"There's that But. You must remove the Buts from your life. Accept the denial, the negative, the rejection, the tragic, and move on. You're a soldier in life, Ann. You are a very significant person. You could hold the truth in your hands."

"Alright. And. And I would love to help you with it, and I will do that if you will take my advice because otherwise it's too maddening to argue with you. And, Griffin, I will not be free from this current workload for at least three days. However. Is that allowed? However?" She chuckled, and Griffin took up the humorous mood, laughing with her, his voice sweet and rough at the same time as he reeled her in on his silver thread of persuasion.

"However can be acceptable, at certain times."

"Then, however, it won't be for a few days. Okay?"

"A couple of days. Maybe just one. How about tomorrow? My door is always open. Call me."

He abruptly hung up, and Ann sat there for a while, wondering what it was she had just been through, why she enjoyed the sparring, and already looked forward to seeing him. She was as needy and crazy as him, for sure. It was time she met someone new.

***

That's when the phone rang again. She shouldn't have picked it up.

"Ann, it can't wait. You know how much you mean...."

"I've heard this before. What's coming?"

"It's bad."

She waited. Feeling the dread creep over her.

"I know she told you about when we met. I've done something really stupid. I trust you to hear me out. Thing is. I fell for her that weekend, that exquisite flower. She was haughty and cold with me. I was just the dealer, the Yank, no more than the help. But I was in love."

He paused. Ann gave him nothing.

"When she spoke her name the other night my heart exploded. But there it was, the same disdain. I wanted to shock and hurt her, make her see me this time. See my power, what I did to them all. My life was haunted for years by her downfall and suffering, but look at her, she survived it and she still looked at me like I was shit. I just couldn't let it go, could I? All the secrecy, and I just blew it away. I'm a fucking idiot. If she tells her friends then there's only trouble for me."

Ann could barely whisper the words. But she had to help him.

"She's not going to tell anyone."

"Can you help me with that? That's what I'm asking."

"I already have. Stop worrying. I have to go."

CHAPTER 34

Ann's Apartment

Ann sat up in bed leafing through the books she'd found in the library, enjoying the new shift in her feelings for Griffin, like a massive weather change, from attachment to detachment. He would be surprised to know he'd released her from their emotional tie with his strange confession. From a distant perspective she was feeling sorry for him now.

Most of the books revealed the scandals of London's swinging sixties. A lot of ground was covered on the titillating Profumo girls, which entertained her for a good hour before she moved on. She'd forgotten the story and learned some new details, horrifying contrasts in fate. There were mentions of some drug busts of individual characters, well known to the public, but none more colorful thanThe Veils' catastrophe, yet none of the writers had bothered to learn more about the focal point in the story, the disappearance of the mystery dealer. Perhaps they'd tried and reached a dead end. Curious. She wondered if the English newspapers of that time were available on file.

One of the newer publications she found at Samuel French was just a glossy collection of photos, a few she hadn't seen before, including an early one of Madeleine and Pete Stebbings. It looked like their first public outing. Ann was touched by how young they looked and she remembered herself. Slim and pale, girlish in those little Biba dresses. That was the year Ann could have become anything, a film actress, a model. She was shy and just beyond mousey but once she put on the eyelashes and pale lipstick lots of lecherous men swept down on her like she was fresh meat.

Tarquin's death took her in another direction. She answered to the call of the Maharishi, then found her own path, through Europe and the Far East, before falling in love with an older man, mentor, screenwriter, alcoholic, and followed him back to London to become his wife. They had a fascinating short life together but she couldn't save him from the decline caused by his creative failures. Fortunately she met everyone in the movie business, and was offered an exciting job in an international literary and talent agency.

After a few painful years of combining happy success, an exhilarating life in the movies, and the sadness of having to leave him, Ann seized the chance to do that by moving to the West Coast. She still carried with her a great vision of the world and a belief that justice was possible. Working inside the Hollywood system instead of Europe took care of that unfortunate illusion, but it enabled her to become a respected writer and widow.

Just before she turned off the light and shoved the books onto the floor, Ann made her plan for tomorrow. She would check the proofs of her story with the newspaper over the phone, lock it in by noon, take a leisurely bath, then have a pleasant lunch with one of her impartial friends who would make her laugh. Then call Griffin and drop by his cave early in the evening, before he got high, and just stay a little while. Hope there

would be no reference to their last conversation.
And not get engaged in a tussle of wills. He
always won. She would be at an advantage by
taking over a pie, a peace offering. Good idea.

CHAPTER 35

Outside Barneys Beanery – West Hollywood - Thursday

Vince had tucked himself into a corner behind a parked truck where he could watch for the arrival of Cortez. He'd told him exactly where to park. Burning a guilty hole in his pants pocket was a small heavy disc which would activate a tracking system by transmitting a signal to a receiving device, very sophisticated stuff, results guaranteed. All he had to do was attach it to the underside of Cortez's car.

The three hours of phoning, persuading and technical tuition Vince had gone through made this last act a triumph of simplicity. He had made a few friends in various useful clandestine professions, with his free tickets, VIP passes and a rare chance to rub shoulders with the famous, all of which he wielded with spare cunning. His buddy Jacko, the owner of this tracking device, was one of them.

Now he was tapping his feet with impatience, blaming himself for arriving way too early, geared up with unfamiliar tension. Relief came with the arrival of an obvious rental snaking into the small car park.

Vince watched the suave black man emerge with a grandeur not appropriate to the vehicle or the occasion, and certainly not the venue. Something about Cortez bothered Vince. The cool attitude, the experienced look of an operator, he didn't trust it. Suddenly he had a thought. Cortez could be an undercover cop, or a private detective, he was so confident in his style. Vince watched Cortez as he strolled out of the car park.

Waited a few beats, then walked over to the rental, dropped a pack of cigarettes on the ground, cursed for effect, bent down to pick them up and attached the bug. He then walked over to a payphone and made a short call to Jacko to signal success, before following his target into the restaurant, where Cortez stood staring around, seeming surprised that Vince was not already there waiting.

Those few seconds were enough for Cortez to get suspicious, annoyed, and righteously offended. He was being stood up. A moment later Vince walked in, looking strangely smug.

The coffee time was pleasant. The two men had started off formal, then steered by Vince with subtle mastery, they talked about the appeal of rock and roll up against rhythm and blues. Vince knew which buttons to push, he'd seen them all in concert. Earth Wind and Fire got Cortez's defenses down, and it wasn't difficult for the two men to connect, just short of ordering a second round. Neither man submitted any useful information about their sources or motivations, so the meeting was something of a standoff. Cortez seemed oblivious to the undercurrents, and Vince was very relaxed anyway, with his little bug in place, observing that Cortez was constantly looking at his watch. Obviously on a schedule.

CHAPTER 36

Outside Ann's Apartment

Cortez couldn't wait to get away from Vince and rejoin the Ann Stapleton stake-out. He had spent all morning outside her apartment, except for the coffee break. He was thankful he'd guessed right about her, that she'd be staying at home today, after that late night at the newspaper and her deadline. He sat in the car musing how involved he was getting with Ann Stapleton because he found himself very happy to see her sauntering down the road to her car at 1:15 pm looking refreshed and lovely. He followed her, almost in a trance, to what turned out to be a late lunch at a place called the Ivy, where she joined an elegant looking black girl at an outdoor table. He wished he had the credentials to follow up on that, but he was confused enough. The restaurant was very popular, even this late, and he was forced to park a distance away, look for a free space coming up, rush to his car then re-park. Was this the real world?

Back in his car outside Ann's, post-lunch, he was getting that anxious grip in his stomach again, wondering if he'd made a big mistake with this crazy gamble. A hunch that could keep him in this whacky town forever. He'd put so much faith into the woman leading him to his target, but he didn't have anything else and doubted that Vince had a clue.

And now, to back it up this time, perhaps, here she was, emerging from her building, carrying a cake box. He tried to marry the image he had of Leonard Rivkin with a cake-bearing angel, but that wouldn't match, so he just got into the car, started up and took off behind the Pacer.

CHAPTER 37

Outside Griffin's Place

Cortez was hyped up, he couldn't remember when he last felt this excited. He felt the power. Ann Stapleton had led him to this strange corner of Los Angeles. He didn't know what the district was called, but the clues were everywhere.

It was a perfect hideout. Once a corner shop in a narrow street off a rundown retail thoroughfare surrounded by cheap beauty supplies, coffee shops, a kosher bakery, a launderette, and a kosher fish market.

The building was screened from pedestrian view and vice versa. The window flanked an obviously unused entrance door, set back and solidly blocked by a rusty iron gate. Locked into the space amongst long accumulated dirt were uncollected rolled up newspapers turning brown, discolored flyers and various bits of street garbage blown into the eternal grime on the cracked tiles.

Armed with an agent's knowledge of a hide-out, Cortez recognized that it was all artfully designed to look both impenetrable and uninviting.

The display window was even more revealing to Cortez. As if casually left behind by a previous tenant were a few dust-covered items. The partial torso of an antique rosy cheeked doll, one set of eyelashes missing, a torn book, an old sepia photo of two kittens in a broken frame. Scattered here and there were long faded blue paper flowers. A cracked plastic Halloween mask grinned dull pink and sinister in one corner, caustic

observer of it all. The weirdo was in there, Cortez
knew. His heart started thumping. He wasn't sure
what to do next. Except wait.

He quickly walked around the whole block,
wanting to avoid going too near the two-story
blank wall that abutted the alleyway, and round to
the front door. Examining the rear from a distance
through his binoculars, he was not surprised to
see what looked like a sensor device above the
rear door and on the adjacent corner. There were
no security cameras, but this was good enough to
detect loiterers.

When he finally arrived back at the far end
of the alley he could see that nothing had
changed. No parked cars had been moved. He
relaxed for a moment, picked up the binoculars
again and studied the area around the back door.
There was an iron grill security gate, now folded
back, and the solid looking door itself carried bits
of paraphernalia, some little stick-on decals for
punk rock bands, he deduced from the aggressive
names, a few printed business cards, curled up at
the edges, and several signs proclaiming the
same theme to any would-be invaders. Private! Go
Away, No Callers, Death to Intruders. The
collected works of a paranoid recluse.

Cortez was very curious about the time
between Rivkin's escape from the safe house, and
holing up in this one where he had evidently spent
a number of years. How and why did he end up
here? Sizing up the space from his exterior
examination, he guessed that the entire two floors
were Rivkin's domain. A well-sealed box with two
exits. Cortez was idly wondering about the roof
access when he saw car headlights coming from a

side road at the far end of the block and turning into the alleyway.

He ducked into a carport and observed an old model Chevy being hurled into a small space with the expertise of a frequent visitor, and a sexy looking woman, who left the car with a loud slam, didn't lock it, and headed straight for Rivkin's back door. She thumped on it, pushed it straight open, closed it behind her, and left Cortez bewildered and loaded with questions. Another woman? An angry one? Plus a very useful observation. The door was very heavy, reinforced, and most likely bullet proof.

Cortez was positively salivating for his prey, but the predator had no choice but to wait some more.

It was less than ten minutes later when another car approached, from the same end of the alley, parked carelessly, and two young guys with Mohawks got out, laughing and talking loudly as they sauntered on their heavy boots, wobbling a bit against each other, and knocked on the door. They didn't wait more than a second before pushing the door open, swallowed by the light inside, then dark silence came over the alleyway once more.

Cortez didn't move from his observation post back in the car. He was rewarded by a sudden surprise when the door burst open and the woman came out, arguing, turning to gesticulate at the man following her, who pulled the door shut and stood there, reasoning with her.

It was him. Too sudden for Cortez. He was glad to be sitting down. Yes, it was him. He couldn't see his face properly, but the body type and manner told him he was looking at an older

Leonard Rivkin. He held his breath and tried to hear their words.

"....make me feel like I'm not wanted."

Rivkin gestured in a conciliatory way and moved toward her, putting out his hand to touch her face. She slapped it away and stalked to her car door, yanking it open.

"Not true, not true. How long has it been like this?"

"Too long."

"That's not what I mean."

This time she allowed him to come closer and slide his arm around her shoulder, the other hand touching her hair.

Cortez couldn't hear the rest, but the couple embraced loosely, swaying a little together, ending with a kiss. Rivkin walked backwards to his door, waving briefly as the car backed out of its space. Watched him slump for a moment as he reached his door, then pull back his shoulders before plunging back in. It was a very private moment.

Instantly Cortez made his move. It was an impulsive decision, and the right one, he was sure of it. He managed to start the car, turn it around and catch up with the woman before she could take a right into the main road, kept nicely out of view and followed her on a very long trek which ended in what he later found out was The Valley. Like a good agent he made notes all the way, street names, store signs, landmarks, and finally her exact address. This was her home, no question about that.

Cortez felt satisfied now he had a second lead, and a more likely connection. He wasn't happy at the work involved, staking out the lady. Following her around to get some background on her life. That was the work he was trained to do, but he was younger then. In those times he would have slipped into a local motel, but he'd paid up at the other one, his personal gear was there and he was desperate for sleep. He just wished he had access to that office computer. Her license plate number wasn't much use to him, but he wrote it in his book.

It was a thirty-five minute drive from her house back to West Hollywood. He had to return again in the early morning. He made his plans and drove away.

CHAPTER 38

Industrial Technical Supplies - Pico Boulevard, Los Angeles

Vince had been watching the little dot that was Cortez's car sit unmoving for hours on the computer screen map at the technology lab. Cortez must have been on a stake out. Particularly a small apartment block Cortez could be watching from his car. Half an hour later the dot moved, taking off towards Sunset; it made a right and then another right and moved rapidly along Fountain Avenue towards Hollywood. The journey was short, ending with some inexplicable turns and coming to a stop in a small street close to Fairfax Avenue.

Vince scrambled to get to the scene. Speeding over to find Cortez wedged down inside his rental, only the top of his head showing as he stared out into the dark alley. It was impossible to tell on the drive past which was the target address.

Vince decided to wait it out, keeping Cortez just visible in the distance. Obviously he'd followed someone to this place. Now Vince watched him watching the arrival first of a woman in a big car; then two punks, apparently stoned, turned up and they all went in the same door.

It wasn't a long wait. A door opened, a woman and a man came out. They seeming to be arguing. She got into her car and swept by looking upset, and Vince just had time to duck out of the glare of headlights as Cortez started up and followed her, passing within inches of Vince's car. .

When it was quiet again Vince got out and walked over to the heavy door covered in crap, looking for a number and address, without any luck.

He had the bright idea of going round the building to what would be the front entrance to find it, avoiding the obvious sensor overhead. He knew it; this was the place where Rivkin lived, and judging by the description Reggie had given him, Vince knew that he had seen the man himself. Mission accomplished.

He bought a bottle of Jack Daniels on the way home in anticipation of celebrating a job well done. Checking the Swindon Lodge tour itinerary, he made the call. Reggie was his usual laid back Brit, but Vince could tell he was very pleased and would no doubt be calling his friend Tony in England with the good news.

CHAPTER 39

Pete's House - Friday

It was early morning and Tony was out in the rear courtyard of the house, polishing the chrome on an old but perfectly shiny red Jaguar XK140, The car was his reason for living. He had an idea he might drive Pete to the airport himself, seeing he had so little luggage, and the Bentley was in the shop. Heard his mother calling him to the phone, it was Los Angeles. Tony tossed the rag away and ran into the house; she was holding it out in her fingers like a biochemical threat.

"Some Englishman. Didn't give his name," she frowned.

"Tony Winston here. Reggie! Good morning old sport, early night?"

"Yes, brother, travel day, we're in New Orleans now. Just got a phone call from our friend in the security business. He found your mystery chap. Want the address?"

Tony reached for a pad and pen, clicking his fingers at Mum, who pushed them towards him and stood there pouting. Tony just turned away and wrote.

"Leonard Rivkin. Right. And? Fairfax, where's that? Oh, I know, where the Farmers Market is. I'm such a Beverly Hills boy, you know. Okay, got it. Two more? Well, give them to me anyway. Anything else on Rivkin? No current name, license plate, I.D. or….Okay, well call it in when you get something. I'll transfer the balance into his account by wire, soon as I hang up. Well done. You came through. I'm sure my party here will appreciate it."

After some brief tour gossip, Tony put the phone down and turned to his mother, who was now watching the kettle boiling, teapot at the ready.

"You seem to be very busy plotting something, my lad. What is it?"

"Oh nothing, Mum, just an old acquaintance of Pete from the sixties who left the scene and he's got unfinished business with him. It's nothing, really."

"Well, pull the other leg, it's got bells on. You and Miss Ping and that sad old wreck from up north, you're all in on something. Look, we worked our fingers to the bone to get some peace and quiet. Now we've got it and you're turning it upside down."

"Just bear with me, Mum, it's almost over and we'll be back to normal."

"I read somewhere that change is growth and growth is change. And I don't like either of them."

"Been reading Pete's books again, Mum?"

"Matter of fact, yes. And I like some of the things I pick up. Better than religion and the Bible as far as clearing up some of the mysteries. Look at us, we've done well and all because you've got a good friend in Pete. You have to take care of him."

"I do, Mum, for crying out loud, I couldn't do more, now, could I?"

"Yes, you could. If he's going to Los Angeles to see this unfinished business, you should be close behind him to cover his backside."

"You think?"

The kitchen intercom rang and Tony picked it up.

"Morning Pete. You're up early. Tea now. Breakfast at 8. Right. Everything's ready, we're going to the airport in the Jag. And guess what, I got the location of that Rivkin fella Madeleine was talking about. One of those odd connections, old friend of Reggie's knew where to put his finger on him. No? Well, I'll put it in your day runner anyway. Okay, she's on the way."

When he was sure Mum was off with the tea tray, Tony picked up the phone and dialed a number.

Carol answered; she was sleepy and depressed.

"Tony!" she brightened. "How're you doing, pet?"

"Well, much better for hearing your voice, sweetheart. How're you?"

"Not very good. Barry's been a real white woman's burden for days now. After his triumphant appearance at your local pub and a couple of days on the other side of the tracks he came down to earth with a thud. Then I realized he'd stopped taking the valium or any of the other ones, just so he could indulge his anger, regret and...what was the other thing?"

"Self-pity?"

"Yeah, that too. Lost the desire to live, he said. I thought that was pretty drastic and I haven't had much sleep but I've been overdosing him with good food and body rubs, got him back on the medication and he's fast asleep upstairs now. Hope I can get some rest. What's up with the rich and famous?"

"Thought you'd like to know I traced Mister X. King Leonard Rivkin now lives in a rundown shop in the Fairfax district, which is a kind of orthodox Jewish enclave with connections to the underground punk crowd who hang out at the local all-night deli."

Carol started writing notes from the conversation on a telephone notepad.

"Well, well. So he's had his comeuppance then. He goes from hanging out with the stars so he can bust them and ruin their lives, to living in a ghetto. Give me the address. I'd like to have it. Just.....you know."

She nodded and wrote down the details.

Out of sight halfway up the second flight of stairs to the bedroom, Barry sat in his dressing gown, listening to every word. When Carol finished and shuffled off to the kitchen, he nipped down, copied the information on another sheet of the pad, tore it off and went back to the bedroom.

CHAPTER 40

Outside Juno's House – Studio City - Friday

Cortez sat in his rented car again, but this time his mood was bright: the hunter lion had the benefit of a good sleep and breakfast, his fine suit enhanced by a new shirt, with his notebook and *Wall Street Journal* on the passenger seat. This was the day his pursuit would be paying off and he loved the anticipation of success.

All he had to do was follow the woman to a place where he could approach her. Win her confidence and get close to that man. He'd been right about Ann Stapleton all along.

He had a clear view of the lady's car where she had parked it the night before, but as the hours passed he lost every bit of confidence and optimism. She never left the house. Cortez was itching with frustration, afraid to leave his post in case he missed her. Even a few minutes could be fatal.

Eventually he gave up. Trying to think methodically. It was no good going back to Ann Stapleton in the hope of using her as an introduction to Rivkin. She was smart. She'd smell a rat. He had to stick with what he was doing. He would give it one more chance tomorrow.

CHAPTER 41

British Airways Flight to Los Angeles-
Friday

Barry was slumped into his window seat, pleased with himself for the alacrity with which he'd transported himself from the staircase at home to a jet bound for L.A.

He believed in going straight to the source, and he'd hurriedly packed a small bag of necessities, tiptoed past Carol in deep sleep on the sofa, out the door, down the road to a taxi stand, a short drive to the station, and the fast train to Newcastle Airport, where he enlisted the help of an efficient little girl at the reservations desk, who found him a perfect set of connections to London and Los Angeles. He took two of his uppers on the train. Dropped by the bank, confirmed that Pete's deposit had cleared and bought some travelers checks. He felt sure God was blessing him, it went so right.

He even got lucky when he phoned Carol, because she didn't pick up and he was able to leave a message, sounding a bit too triumphant but he knew he was in trouble anyway, so what the hell.

Not at all anxious about his plans at the other end. He'd improvise, rent an airport car and go straight to Rivkin's place, park, wait and stalk. He had enough street cred and was familiar with the lowlife habitats of the town. Confident he would find someone who could assist him with the next part of the operation. It would cost him but he'd have plenty when he cashed his travelers checks.

The plane droned on as Barry felt the downers take over from the uppers. Finally he dozed off.

CHAPTER 42

Outside Juno's House - Saturday

Cortez arrived promptly at 7 a.m. and observed the lady's car, still parked at the side of the road. He guessed she must have a lot of junk in the garage. He felt very sour about her this morning, but had prepared himself with his notebooks and the *Wall Street Journal*, and this time he had a couple of sandwiches with him. The hunter lion was surly and restless, but he knew he could master his mood if and when necessary.

When she emerged, around 9:15, the woman seemed to be in a contrastingly sluggish state, probably hadn't slept well, he deduced. Her face was glum as she wandered over to her car and started it up, not looking around as she took off. Cortez followed her for several blocks leading to the busy local boulevard, keeping close enough to watch her pull into an alleyway off the main street, and park in a rear lot shared by a number of shops. He rounded the block and came in behind her, driving to a far spot and staying in his car until he saw her unlock and enter the rear door of a small shop, marked by a cute sign naming it Juno.

Cortez took his time. Strolling around to the main street with the *Journal* under his arm to stop for some fruit at the market. Then he wandered up to the front of the shop and stood there, thoughtfully studying the name and window display, while he picked at the grapes. This was truly a gift from God, assuming God was still on his side in the venture. Juno was a store specializing in underwear and other decorative apparel for large busted ladies.

Setting a sparkle into his brown eyes and a small shit-eating grin on his lips, Cortez strolled in and pretended to look around at the various displays.

The woman was in her late forties, he guessed, sexy and needy he could tell with just one glance. He smiled warmly at her and gave a little wave, continuing his intense study of camisole tops and large sized lacy bras.

"Looking for something for your girlfriend?"

Cortez suppressed a grin. She must have noted his lack of a wedding ring. Smart lady.

"Maybe," he let the grin take over.

"Maybe buying, or maybe girlfriend?"

This was going to be easy.

"Well, if I don't have one now, I'm sure there must be one on the way. A lingerie store called Juno could be a sign. I'm thinking of getting something in anticipation. What do you suggest?"

Juno swayed towards him from behind the counter. Up close she was a dish for an experienced man who knew there was more for him in this vintage model than some skinny adolescent. And Cortez was one of those. He also knew just how much to use this contact and how much to keep it in check until he got what he wanted. He was thinking lunch in that small bistro a few doors down would be the next move, but it was too early for that.

"Sounds like you don't have a specific size in mind. Just a vision?"

She was sounding him out nicely.

"That's right. Something adaptable in terms of size…"

"Then I hope you've got some time to spare because I can make several suggestions. Let's start with these teddies. One size fits all, well not quite all, just the lucky ones."

Cortez joined her at the racks as she carefully plucked out one tantalizing garment at a time and waved it slowly in front of him.

He was just enjoying this and the clear progress in their new friendship when he heard the shop doorbell tinkle and thought, damn, this customer will interfere with the flow. But in walked another lady of the same age, and the two greeted each other with warm glee.

"How're you feeling today, honey?" asked the new arrival. "I won't hug you in case it's catching."

"Oh no, it's just that migraine again, I swear I couldn't stand up. Couldn't sleep either. Thanks for taking care of the place. Sorry it was so quiet."

"Suits me, Juno, I just enjoyed reading my book and did some tidying in the back. I closed early but it was a nice change to be out of the house for a while," she said, looking over at Cortez.

Good, they were best friends. And now he knew why he'd lost an entire day waiting outside her house yesterday. Now all Cortez had to do was spread around his good vibes and take them both out to lunch. It was better. This way he wouldn't be in danger of getting too intimate with Juno, now he knew that was her name, and the women would compete for his attention, so he could expand on the new relationships and get himself over to Rivkin's place faster. Maybe even this afternoon. He was still working on the right motivation, spinning ideas as he went along. He had a lot of wasted time to make up for but he knew he mustn't appear to be in a rush.

Shirley was eager to know more about him, bolder than Juno, and he basked in the attention. They could tell he wasn't a local.

"Are you from New York?" she asked, pointing at the paper.

"No, Florida."

"Oh. But interested in the market I bet."

"In a way. I've always been in broadcasting, but recently I shifted to movies and television. Formed my own production company and just got some funding."

"Oh, that's really exciting," said Juno, stepping forward.

"Hope so. I'm here in L.A., looking for screenplays."

"You must meet a friend of mine. He's a screenwriter, very imaginative."

"Your ex, you mean, some friend," mocked Shirley, as Juno glared at her.

"Oh, ignore her, I can't stand him either, but he's a good writer."

Cortez chuckled. Instinct told him they were talking about Rivkin.

"Is it worth discussing over lunch?" he asked.

There was a moment of awkward silence.

"I'm inviting both of you. Any place you want," he said, raising both arms in a grand gesture.

Shirley laughed and Juno answered.

"We'd be delighted."

CHAPTER 43

Griffin's Place

Rivkin's ominously armed door threw out an aggressive don't come near me ray which made Cortez unusually uncomfortable and nervous even in the full light of day. He was accustomed to high degrees of danger with deliberate risk taking, but this was different.

He examined his feeling as a professional, in order to assess how to cope with what was coming next. It was fear he felt, dark and hostile like the door. Of course. He was on his way to facing the man who'd killed someone he'd admired and wanted to emulate, a skilled agent who had somehow made a fatal error. What kind of man was behind that door, he wondered, someone who killed, ran, and did the almost impossible, managed to hide from investigation and pursuit all these years.

Cortez forced the image away and focused on the person these two women had described to him. A struggling writer, a brilliant storyteller, a lovable if foolish man who was working on an exciting visionary screenplay. He formed a warm loose smile and crinkled his hard brown eyes as Juno pushed the door open and he met the sharp blue ones of the man at the top of the stairs.

The shock pulled Cortez back instinctively and he was afraid he might have betrayed himself with his reaction. He saw Rivkin dart some meaningful glares at the two women then do a snap top-to-toe evaluation of him. Not a good start, Cortez thought as he stepped towards Rivkin, following the two women who greeted him with the brushing hugs and lip pursing that passed for affection in L.A. Cortez made an effort and offered a handshake which Rivkin was slow to accept.

"Hi, Calvin is it? Calvin what? Juno said you're a producer."

Rivkin was bouncing on the balls of his feet like a boxer, showing some energy, probably to make up for not being as tall as any of his three visitors. He flicked ash off his cigarette, took a pull at it and shot another blue laser at Cortez, this time squinting a bit and twitching his mouth into a very small grudging smile. He suddenly changed to a welcoming mode and ushered Cortez to a large wing armchair that dominated the small space.

"Here, have a chair, man. Sorry, just woke up a while ago. Heavy night."

"Calvin Robert Cortez. Yeah, I'm from Florida, great place to raise money and make movies. Not such a good place to find the screenplays we want, so…"

"So, you found anything yet?"

"I'm reading a few, trying to get more meetings with good agents. It seems to be a very tight place, Hollywood. I should have spent more time and money on getting column inches for myself and my company before I got here. But I prefer to meet the writers personally. Apart from the top guys, I get the impression there are two kinds of writers, those with agents who can't sell their scripts, and those who are looking for agents and can't get them to open the first page. Where do you stand on that?"

Rivkin looked wary and alert again. He obviously didn't like being questioned and was touchy on the subject of agents. He behaved as if he were surrounded by strangers, which Cortez thought odd, as Juno was his ex-wife, and he'd supposedly known Shirley for years. It was clearly habitual paranoia, the edgy behavior of a man on the run, in hiding, guilty and on guard.

"No agent. You got that part right. I've been let down by a few people I thought I could trust with my work. Which is of the most paramount importance, to me and to the world. You ever been an agent?"

Cortez's eyes flickered at the question, he felt it and knew Rivkin saw it too.

"Hell no. I was in radio for many years, went through the system from sweeping the floors to disc jockey to buying the station and then a few others. They did well. I had an affinity with behind the scenes and I always had a yen to get into films, so I made the moves, the right ones, and now I've got the funding to go into probably three movie productions over the next two years. I want to be Jerry Bruckheimer."

"Yeah, and what about his partner?"

"No, I don't want to be him. And I don't need a partner. What's your story about?"

"Action adventure. Background story's a plot situation concerning something major that's coming down in the future. Rock the world big time."

"Science fiction?"

"No. Didn't Juno tell you anything about it?"

"Not a thing. She only told me you had a good story, and a movie that would bring in a big audience. That's the basic element I'm looking for.

With some intelligence in there too. You don't have to tell me right now if you don't want to. I could just read it."

"Well.....that might not be exactly what I want to do right now. I'm keeping a lot of the detail under wraps. It's sensitive. I'm the receiver and guardian of some significant vital information, which I'm using in this story, you understand. No, you don't understand. It's the sort of material Langley would want to know about. You know what Langley is?"

"No, is it a movie company?"

"You could say that, it's a company and it's a place. Never mind."

Cortez felt a veil of sweat oozing from his forehead, and tried to relax. He sat back in the chair and crossed his legs, moving his face away from the yellow flare of the lamp beside him. By contrast his mind was working fast, his voice still casual.

"I can understand your being careful about material. There's a lot of plagiarism potential in movies. Did you register it with the Writers Guild?"

"Sure thing. You smoke?"

"Na, gave it up years ago."

"No, I meant one of these," said Rivkin, waving a rolled joint he seemed to have plucked out of nowhere. He flicked his lighter, lit up, pulled a very deep chestful of smoke, and deftly turned it around in his hand to pass it across to Cortez. It was one of those significant moments that can make or break a stake-out. Cortez took it and grinned with pleasure at the joint before drawing on it himself.

"My, this is a welcome sight. Nice to know you, Griffin."

He coughed a little, and laughed. As he let go of his own shoulders, he could see Rivkin also relax and let his blue eyes twinkle.

"Now I really feel I'm on the West Coast."

Rivkin accepted the tribute and waved for Cortez to take another toke. He breathed in the joint, holding it awkwardly, coughing some more as he let it all out. Cortez passed it to Juno, who took a long draw on it before passing it to Shirley.

The atmosphere in the room noticeably changed. Rivkin was still on his feet, laughing now but still watching the other three with the eyes of a hawk. The pot had loosened them all, and Cortez figured that Rivkin was ready to open up.

Wrong. Rivkin was suddenly behind him holding a gun to his head. Cortez was so surprised he did the unthinkable. Swiveling his head around at the touch of the metal, to look up into the blue-grey barrel.

"You're a spook, man, I can tell. I can smell spook. What the hell are you doing, bringing him into my house?" Rivkin hissed at Juno, who sat rigid and petrified, as Shirley gasped and grabbed a hold of her friend's arm.

CHAPTER 44

Cortez stayed calm and strong. He was in known territory now and confidence flooded back into him in an instant.

"Mr. Griffin, please. Whatever it is you think I am, I can assure you I am not. Now...Put the gun away. Please."

"What's the matter with him?" shrieked Shirley. "Is he a racist? He's sick. Juno, get me out of here. I don't want trouble, I've got a husband to take care of."

Juno sat up straight in her chair, her stare fixed on Rivkin, her voice strong and unwavering. Cortez could see with some relief that she was familiar with this role and this scene.

"Lennie, if you don't put that gun away, I swear I'm never coming here again, and you know what that means. None of us are going to call the police. Just remove the gun from that man's head and put it down on the desk. Right now, Lennie. Lennie!"

Slowly Rivkin lowered his arm and stepped backwards, found the desk behind him and put down the gun, keeping his hand close.

Cortez carefully let his breath out and heard his heart pounding as he got up and gingerly but expertly maneuvered his way towards the door as he spoke.

"Let's forget all this happened. Just pretend I never came here, right? I would have been very interested in your script but obviously we're not compatible, if that's what you want to call it. Hey, I thought you wanted to get your movie made."

Shirley was already on the way out, edging quickly past Rivkin in the narrow room and leaping up the stairs to join Cortez at the door. Juno stopped on the way to confront Rivkin and spit parting words at him, giving Cortez and Shirley the opportunity to leave.

"You fucking fool, look what you've done. You blew another chance, you don't want to get anywhere. You just want to rot here like a cockroach, afraid of the whole world."

"Look what *you've* done, bitch, bringing that stranger here. You swallowed his line. What do you know? I know. I can tell a government man from a mile away. You're so gullible. You're supposed to be protecting me, helping me with my work, my path in life. You want to find me a producer? Find me a real one."

"There's nothing wrong with him, you're just terminally paranoid and I'm sick of it."

"There are six ways I could tell that guy's a fake."

"Yeah? Name one."

"Shoes."

"Shoes? You're crazy. I'm outta here. Forget me ever trying to make something happen for you and your lousy writing, and stinking life."

"Secondly by the way he handled the smoke. Those guys don't go near a joint, they never know when there'll be a mandatory piss test. Probably his first time."

"That's it, you lost me. Goodbye."

Rivkin reached out for her. She shrugged him off and ran up the stairs, heaving the door shut behind her.

Outside, still running, she caught up with Shirley and Cortez, who was already in his car, revving the engine, Shirley standing by the window, trying to calm herself.

"Look, I mean it," said Cortez to Juno. "I want to just forget that whole scene. I should call the cops, I know, but that won't help anyone. So , forget it."

He could see Juno was ready to jump in with a stream of excuses.

"Don't try to explain, he's a drug casualty. Dangerous to you and himself. Drugs and guns are bad but he's paranoid and that's a triple play."

"I'm really sorry. I'm embarrassed."

"Like I said, I'm forgetting the whole thing and so should you. Now please go to Shirley's, at least till he calms down."

Shirley nodded at Juno, and took her arm.

"He's right, Juno, you can stay in the spare room as long as you like."

Cortez stared hard at Juno now, making sure she got it. He was anxious to get this over and make his next move.

" Go there and stay, don't answer the phone, don't even pick up your car at the store. And we'll just write everything off except the great lunch and some pleasant shopping, huh?"

Both the women were crying now and Shirley put an arm around Juno's shoulder as she led her over to the car. Cortez watched their backs, and counted time, waiting for them to take off so they could all drive away together, Shirley's car in the lead. He wanted to follow the women for a few blocks, to make certain they were far away when it all went down.

CHAPTER 45

Rivkin swiftly moved around his small space, taking a supply of bullets from a box on a high bookshelf, then checking a secret drawer at the back of his desk containing some papers, pulling them out and pushing it back to a concealed position.

Next he grabbed a few bags of marijuana and packets of coke from behind a row of audio tapes, put them into a black leather satchel, like a doctor's bag and added the gun, then opened a cupboard and took out a long black overcoat and a black trilby hat.

He threw the coat on and arranged the hat on his head, letting loose some shiny ringlets of black hair from an attached wig, transforming him into an orthodox Hassidic Jew. Completing the outfit with a large traditional white and black trimmed scarf, and some wire-rimmed spectacles.

Skirting around all the boxes and furniture at the back of the room, he undid locks and padlocks on the shop door, making sure not to disturb the thick surface dust, and locked everything behind him, doing the same moves with the rusty iron gate, scuffling with one foot the old papers and junk, leaving the whole area as if untouched for years. Lastly he pulled out a false beard from his coat pocket, fluffed up the hairs and attached it to his chin by hooking the ends into his false hair.

He'd been waiting for this day. Planning for it. Now it had come.

Rivkin hunched his shoulders, and walked briskly over to the café across the main street, took a table with a newspaper and sipped his coffee as the distant sound of police sirens echoed.

He blithely studied the paper but his mind was racing. Did he take everything, what did he leave behind, where should he go, could he get hold of enough cash to run. Possibly forever.

He took some deep breaths and joined the other staring eyes as three black and whites and a swat truck pulled in to cover the building he had recently vacated. His heart pumped, but he calmly turned to search out the waitress and lifted a finger for her attention. Asking for a menu. Quite happy to commit to an early dinner.

Rivkin wasn't a mindfucker for nothing. He knew that now he was not only invisible on Fairfax but almost inviolable. They wouldn't see him because they wouldn't dare mess with one of them. Wouldn't dare create an incident. There were three other Hassidic men having some dinner, and it was not possible to tell the difference between the real and the fake at this distance. The former King Leo had a lifetime of playing this game.

Ordering the lox, cream cheese and scrambled egg special, he sat back and went on with his orderly planning. The truth was they'd found him. He shouldn't have believed they'd gone away after murdering Billy. Seemed they were convinced they had the right guy then, he thought, and that was two years ago. But they'd kept the door open, someone was still on alert, always had been. But who gave him up?

There were two new people who knew about him. Just a week ago, less, he'd told

Madeleine, and she'd told Ann, he knew that now, and he'd told Ann even more. She wouldn't let him down now he'd confided in her.

In the distance, like a dream, he could hear the stentorian voice over a bullhorn, demanding that Mister Rivkin come out, with his hands in the air. Movies and television made these scenes almost familiar, but when they were actually happening it wasn't any more real. It was surreal. He adopted the same kind of interest in the drama as his fellow diners, but not more. He wanted to blend in.

Rivkin cleared his throat. He had business to take care of. He'd go straight to Ann's place, check it out for the law first. She'd have to hide him, she'd be too scared not to. Besides, she was in love with him, he was sure of that.

Rivkin got his fork to work on the special, savoring the tastes while watching the movement around the front exit of his home. Men were leaning over to study the locks close up, and shaking their heads over the debris in the area between the abandoned gate and door. He wondered if they had now broken into the back door and whether he should have bolted it from the inside to frustrate them.

He shook his head in sad wisdom. He hated always being right about certain things, like recognizing the enemy, especially when people didn't listen. But he was never wrong. That's why he was still alive, and Billy wasn't. As the mysterious guru writer producer, Griffin, he was never interviewed nor photographed, so Billy, his on-camera spokesman, became the target.

As Rivkin mused into his past, he saw Cortez coming round from the alleyway.

CHAPTER 46

Cortez turned his head like a uniformed Roman general to survey the territory in an all-embracing stare, and the other heads followed, all of them taking in the vast area of Fairfax with its characteristic crowded sidewalks and assorted shops. They weren't even thinking disguise yet. These well trained cops didn't know they were being challenged by the Joker, the Trickster, Mistra Know It All. King of Hallucination and Dark Dreams.

Rivkin watched Cortez take charge. Even with the tense scary part that was coming, as the arms of the law were pointing and orders were given, and the group of eight cops went off in their designated directions, with Cortez marching in a direct line to the café with two cops on his heels, Griffin was confident.

As Cortez entered the café, he took out a folded eight by ten of something from inside his coat pocket. Shit, that's a picture of me, said Rivkin's brain to his brain via every organ in his body. Where'd he get that? He knew then they'd been inside his place and looked through his stuff.

His stomach tightened up when he saw Cortez barking at the stringy blonde part-time extra at the cash register, and heard her very loud answer.

"Like that but twenty years older? Give me a break, I don't look at them, I just serve them food."

After the beard, ringlets and glasses, what was left of Rivkin's face was deep in the coffee cup when they scanned him. He returned a critical glance which went with his disguise, as the black man's eyes swept over him without a flicker.

Rivkin kept on staring at the same column in the *Los Angeles Times* business section until he was sure, by the door closings and protracted silence that the law had moved on. Finally he looked up.

A similar sweep was moving up and down the street, the cops panning out and Cortez leading his posse, the Armani jacket flapping in the light breeze.

Rivkin accepted more coffee from the waitress. He had all the time in the world. Now he had to gear up to be Griffin and deal with Ann. She was still his friend, convinced him Madeleine would keep his secret. But that lady was back in London. Could she by lying? Lying to Ann? But what did Juno have to do with it, maybe he'd overlooked something. The couple had been committed to their pledge for eleven years. Why now? Had she reached that point when she could betray him just to be as cruel to him as he was to her? It was a consideration.

He considered the possibility for just a few minutes. Enough for him to be convinced she was genuine and had no idea that Cortez was anything but what he'd presented himself to be. He'd conned her, talked the sweet talk, the lies that came out as poetry to a woman like Juno, still hot between the legs at any time of the day. Not the nights any more after the four glasses or more of wine and a sleeper.

That's it, Griffin had a clear picture. The man had gone to her shop and Shirley was always in there, nothing else to do with that poor old scrawny bastard lying there at home with his mouth open and tubes up both nostrils. Cortez had conned them. Wanting to help old Lennie, and also keep the stud around for a while longer, maybe end up having dinner and a horny hump, guaranteed to give her those noisily eruptive orgasms she favored.

So the guilt was off her now, she had been targeted herself. But how did the Fed know about Juno? Rivkin waved for more coffee and puzzled hard over the question. Had he found Rivkin's place and followed her to the shop from there? Or followed someone else there. Maybe Ann? He was sure Ann was innocent of this. But it had to start somewhere. Someone had triggered this off. And that someone knew some history. Rivkin had never slipped up on keeping that episode in his past a secret. Only Juno knew the truth.

A bad thought jumped into his head as he remembered the photo he showed Madeleine just a few nights ago. Did it have something to do with him? It could if Madeleine told him about the photo. The man whose angry face came up on his personal brain scan video at least once a month. Pete Stebbings. Surely not. But it was possible. Pete Stebbings' revenge, here and now? God....he could get himself killed if he didn't come up with a good plan.

CHAPTER 47

Ann's Apartment

When ann saw the distorted face of a Hassidic Jew in the fishbowl of her front door peephole she froze. Then she saw the mouth moving in an effort to communicate, followed by a hand ripping off a false beard and glasses, then those familiar blue eyes. It was Griffin. He had been here only once before. She opened the door and asked.

"What are you doing here?"

He walked in, shrugged off the big coat, and took off the wig and hat. Tossing them on a chair then wiped the sweat off his face. She had never seen Griffin so obviously frightened.

"I'll get you some water," she offered. Sit down and relax."

"I need vodka, and I can't relax."

Ann came back from the kitchen with the bottle, ice, glasses and water on a tray. Placing it in front of him.

Griffin tossed back the vodka and wiped his chin.

"Jesus. I got a swat team over there. In my own home. I can't go back."

"Start from the beginning."

"When's that? Years or hours ago?"

Ann looked at the vodka and her watch. She poured one for herself over a handful of ice. Determined not to indulge him for once. Just sat there, rattling the rocks around, waiting for him to put his story together.

"My wife brought this man over to my place, he was looking for trouble. You know I have an unusual friendship with my wife."

Ann's eyes swung up, the message clear. "Just get on with it, Griffin."

"Please be kind to me, Ann. I've been through a terrible experience, and I've come to you as a friend."

He cleared his throat roughly as he waited for a sympathetic gesture. There was none.

"She said he was a producer from Miami looking for screenplays, she believes in my work," he continued

"Did you pull a gun on him?"

Griffin threw his arms in the air.

"Yes, as a matter of fact I did. But there was a reason. He was threatening me. You see, I have enemies from the past."

"I know about your past, Griffin, some of it. It's time for you to tell me more about these enemies. "

His face crumbled, like a small boy who'd been found out. But his relief was obvious. He was almost pleading with his eyes for her to take over. Take over the story, take over him. Make everything safe again. She knew this was her role, and that he was near tears. She felt sorry for him.

"I understand now why you blew it that night with Madeleine, and she'll never hear about it from me. But she didn't have to tell me anything. I know you've got your reasons to be paranoid."

"Didn't I always say that?"

"Yes, but you've been living a lie. And now it's all coming back to get you. Where did this guy come from?"

"I knew right off he was FBI. They've never stopped looking for me. That's the truth. I'm still not safe. Even here. He might know about you and where you live but I had nowhere else to go. This has something to do with that night and your friend. She must have informed on me."

"She's not like that."

"You think it's a coincidence? What did she tell you that night?"

"That you were Mister X and I shouldn't see you anymore."

"That all?"

"It was enough. Griffin, what you don't know is that there was a young man you met in London, called Tarquin, who introduced you to Barry and Pete. He was my boyfriend, and he died. She didn't have to give me any details."

Griffin's mouth dropped. He was stunned. For a few seconds Ann held the power over him. She took her time and smiled without warmth.

"Now we know the beginning. Tell me the rest of it."

CHAPTER 48

Griffin reached over to the table for a refill. The bottle clicked against the glass in his shaking hands. He didn't try to show any composure. He had completely lost it and seemed to welcome the change from his usual vain self-promotion. When he looked up, Ann could see his eyes were close to brimming. He let out a huge sigh as if he'd dropped a burden.

"You can't know what it's like to be able to talk about this. I've kept my silence for years, can't trust anybody. They rolled me out of London, you remember the Fleet Street headlines, I was a wanted man. What I knew about certain people behind the scenes was too revealing. The acid. It wasn't just a casual thing. I was supposed to be getting close to some other big names there. You can guess which ones. The Veils were just a start, kind of an experiment. Easy pickings. Pete Stebbings was a sucker for a good high."

"My own intentions were different," he continued. " I believed in encouraging the creative minds of young people in the sixties, they didn't have to get over the fifties like we did. I felt they could be pioneers in world politics, it was all opening up to us. We could have turned it all around. Got rid of racism, hate, guns, be aware we're all one on this planet, work together to make the good life. But money rules, money has other plans. They had me in a noose. Want to know why?"

Ann shrugged. She was very curious now, but knew her silence would draw him out.

"I got busted. Coming in to the U.K. from France. I met this wild man down in Marbella. Dutch. He was mixing some acid, getting to the real deep thing. We thought it could make some money in London. They pulled us over walking through Customs, must have had the look, well he did, that's for sure. They found our hash, then we got the third degree and I was given an option. They told me they were impressed with my act, the smooth talk, even though it failed me. I was to be the dealer, my role was to infiltrate. Don't you love that? They needed a snitch who could get into the top circles."

Ann was trying not to interrupt, but her look of exasperation was loud and clear.

"Alright, alright, you're looking at me like that again. 'They' were government of course. U.S. of A. Call it mind control. One agent had a running mouth, hard-nosed guy and cocky, he told me a lot. Like how else are you going to shut down on a lot of opinionated young liberal thinkers, with loose tongues and masses of media attention? Get them busted of course. Threaten their ability to make money and flaunt their celebrity, turn the business guys against them. Those working class English, they were comets. The idea of losing all that fame and glory was shocking, so they backed off, no more activism. Brilliant scheme. It ruined a few individuals, but the kids got turned on. Get busted and be a hero. But that came later."

"The product was officially launched. It was the sudden drug supply that was the give-away. I was out of the country by then. Hiding in some lousy 'safe house', what a joke. They took my passport, all my I.D.'s, told me I had to go into a witness protection program. More like jail.

Naturally I didn't hold back on my, er, criticism of what they were doing. They were promoting LSD, they had the acid ready to supply the masses. Fried brains don't make for effective revolutionaries. They hated me. I had become their albatross. I knew too much, and I wasn't in the program. They questioned me all the time. Wouldn't give me any peace from it."

Griffin stopped and stared into the distance, puckering his face at the memory.

"Then these other goons showed up at the facility. I could read them from the moment they walked in the door. CIA. Serious interrogation coming up, had to protect myself by acting dumb. I had my cover worked out. Told them I had accidentally overdone a trip. The bottle had tipped over in the fridge and leaked on to some food I had down there, chocolate cake I think I said, took the whole hit. What a story, I started to believe it. I faked my loss of memory, blackouts, failure to co-operate. Came up with a ruse or two to back it up. One time I was smoking a cigarette during an interrogation. One of many. I got the idea on the spot. Just let the cigarette keep burning between my two fingers. Stared into space and made myself drool a bit. Cigarette kept burning, fingers started to smoke, the flesh was sizzling. I just kept staring. They finally snatched it out of my hand and took care of the burn. Jesus, it was my finest moment. Never forget it. See, still got scars."

Griffin reflected on this and Ann allowed him the silence. She'd never seen this side of the man before. He'd made her imagine vividly how he must have felt, and she solemnly closed the gap, taking a swig from the vodka.

"Why were they interrogating you?"

"Some papers they claimed were missing. Nothing to do with me."

"Which means it was, and you took something important to them."

"Okay, yes. But I needed some future leverage. Seized the chance when I saw a file during the early days I was there in the safe house. It was my file actually, there it was, it spilled the beans on their whole plot. Like we say, there are no secret conspiracies, it's all written down if you know where to look."

"What happened next?"

"I stayed in that mode until they gradually classified me as harmless and put me in a different place, gave me a new name, I.D. papers and paid less attention. They got too confident and I found the escape hatch. It took some planning, preparations, furtive research, enjoying the challenge, I watched Stalag 17 on TV one night, it was all about detail and patience."

Griffin's eyes began to glow as he jumped to his feet and started to pace, his old self again.

"Ann, you know I trust you completely. It's a relief to share this, never done it before. This must go no further."

This time it was an order, not a request.

"Griffin, you're being ridiculous. This is a very serious situation and you're still trying to entertain me. Give it up."

"Why? Not much time left."

He dropped back into the chair again and finally said, "I'm exhausted."

"Then sleep. Not here. I'll take you to my neighbor's place, down the hall, she's away and I'm feeding her cats. Come on."

She took him by the arm and led him out of her apartment and down the corridor to a door, which she quickly unlocked and opened. Guiding him inside and directly to the bed, shoving him down with a touch. She removed his worn-out sneakers as if they were toxic, covered him up with the quilt and studied him for a moment.

"Will they come for you with guns blazing?"

He shook his head solemnly. "They'll try to be subtle at first but they're relentless. You have to stay consistent with the same story. You haven't seen me since whenever, I never come over here, don't even know where you live. Just stick to it. My God, my stuff."

"I'll get it. You just sleep, no noise."

Griffin let out a sigh when he heard the door click again as Ann left after dumping his rabbi disguise and bag. His mouth twitched sideways as he considered the absurdity of it all and fell asleep.

CHAPTER 49

The Mondrian Hotel, West Hollywood

Pete finished checking into his hotel room with the casual polish of a veteran, palming notes into the hands of each of the attendants, bell boys, luggage carriers, far too many of them as usual, but of course they all wanted to take a good look at Pete Stebbings.

He pulled out his few essentials, toilet bag, a couple of books, his day runner, dressing gown and slippers, then he threw himself back on the bed and relaxed for a few minutes, doing some full deep breaths.

Rose from the bed and did some toe touching and stretching, cracked a few fingers, and plucked up the day runner, reaching for the phone at the same time. He flipped to his "To Do" list, already in the process of activating No. 1, as he dialed his home number, and didn't have to wait for more than two rings, house rule, before Tony answered.

"Tony, I'm here, Room 710, what's up?"

"Nothing, guv. Quiet as church on cup tie."

"Good stuff. Well, I've got my itinerary to keep me busy. Just if there's a call from the New York record company, buzz me right away, okay?"

Now Pete was on the phone again, this time waiting patiently for someone to locate Ann at the paper, No. 2 on his list, complete with phone number and address.

"She doesn't come in on Fridays."

"Can you give me another number then, please, it's Pete Stebbings here. I'm an old friend from London. I'll be gone by Monday."

"Oh? Oh, sure, Pete. It's 659.3729."

"That must be near here. I'm at the Mondrian."

"Yes, just round the corner, down on Alta Loma, 1122, it's the condo building just by Holloway."

"Oh thanks, perfect. I appreciate your help."

Pete didn't wait for the unctuous response. He hated it that Americans were so personal right off like that, with the Oh Sure, Pete. Couldn't they just say Mister Stebbings sometimes, it pissed him off.

Now Pete had to do some thinking. His To Do List was becoming redundant, and he contemplated phoning Ann but decided to go for the dramatic effect. In short time he had changed his outfit, ordered the car up from the garage, checked his cash, and pulled out a small bottle of iced white wine from the bar fridge. He threw a lightweight jacket over his arm, concealing the bottle, pocketed his wallet and took off, with a certain strut of anticipation in his step. Jesus, he thought, L.A. is certainly a high, after good old lollabout England. This was exciting.

CHAPTER 50

Ann's Apartment

Ann felt satisfied with the way the interview was going. She knew the detective was convinced with her story. She had given him that straight-faced combination of helpful truth and downright lies that she had acquired as a skill from her years in the movie business, handling artists and producers. Making a subtle point of referring to Griffin by the name she knew, and being surprised at the name the man used for him.

She decided to add to her credibility by wondering why she'd never heard his real name before. Cortez was casual about his explanation, guessing that in this world of everybody being their own artwork the man had chosen a more colorful professional name for himself. After all, the Griffin logo was everywhere on his work, on the walls of his apartment and the tiny fetishes lying around.

Ann was pretty sure that this was the same man Griffin had described as the FBI agent pretending to be interested in his scripts. She was surprised at first to see he was black, funny how people, even Griffin, never mentioned it. He was also sophisticated and literate, not that unusual, but he had a kind of intimate charm that tweaked her as a woman, and she was enjoying it.

"So you're saying you haven't seen him in the last twenty-four hours?

"No, I haven't," she answered.

Now her problem was that he didn't seem to want to leave, so she offered him a drink, knowing that a cop wouldn't accept alcohol on the job. She smiled when he declined and made moves for the door.

"May I call you in a few hours to see if everything's alright here?"

"Of course, any time. Here's my card. You have one?"

"I don't, but let me write a number down for you."

Ann smiled again as she watched him carefully write his number on a small notepad he kept in the inside pocket of his jacket. Obvious, he didn't want her to know who he really was. Griffin's threatening spook theory seemed valid suddenly.

Cortez withdrew politely, after a last thorough scan of the room, and she waved sweetly, thinking of Griffin, asleep just a few yards away.

Cortez trotted down the stairs, feeling the necessity to scope out the exits from this lady's apartment. She was soft and sharp at the same time, that English skin and a mischievous smile. She had to be over forty but she was sexy—very sexy. And maybe a damn good liar.

He had no idea what to do next, but he wasn't going to reveal that to the local cops waiting in the street. Cortez figured that Rivkin had a network of underground wasters, losers and suspicious punks, and could be hiding out with any one of them, in any cave or rat hole from here to downtown. He felt defeated at the prospect, but he was very close to the man he'd been tracking for so long, and now wasn't the time for defeat.

Maybe the lady upstairs was a bit too smooth about everything. Maybe he should go back without any advance warning. He almost turned around. Decided against it and kept walking.

CHAPTER 51

Griffin's Place

Pete slowly navigated his rental car into the narrow unmarked alleyway he'd missed the first time around, and parked between two cars that looked deceased. He sat quietly, calming himself.

He'd thought about getting a gun, but that wasn't what he wanted. In fact he wouldn't know what he really wanted until he was face to face with The Acid King.

There was no doubt Rivkin would recognize him, who would forget a face like his, but he had a new thought as he slowly approached the door and saw the peephole. If Rivkin was as paranoid as he should be then he might not even open it. He knocked for the fifth time and heard no sounds coming from inside. Damn, he was deflated now. He hadn't allowed for this. He stood dangling on the doorstep for a few minutes more before going back to his car. Major encounter number one would have to be postponed, now it was on to major encounter number two, something he actually looked forward to. And the wine would still be cold.

***

Cortez was on his way back to the crime scene, driving along Fountain and steeling himself to call Juno and Shirley when the transmitter burped. His senses came back to life when he heard the stake-out cop's voice.

Swear to God, it was Pete Stebbings, the English rocker."

"I heard you the first time, Sergeant, and I believe you. What I mean is what the hell is he doing there? And why right now?"

"Well, just guessing, but from where we were parked he looked like an innocent visitor. He couldn't have known what went down there this afternoon. He must be an old friend, and just dropped by. Coincidence."

"Okay, get someone on him. He should be in a hotel, try all the obvious ones. I know he lives in England, so check the airlines over the last couple of days. See if he just flew in. Whatever else you can think of. There must be a lead in here somewhere."

Cortez congratulated himself; he'd made the right decision, clearing away the crime scene tape and any evidence of cops. Hoping that Rivkin might just be confident enough to return to his home when it got dark. He decided to just sit and wait.

CHAPTER 52

Ann's Apartment

One more time ann had an amazing experience through the peephole of her front door. Pete Stebbings?

Standing there, wearing a three-piece suit with no tie, a light Italian mac, and holding a bunch of flowers, with an unwrapped bottle of white wine dripping in his fist.

"You look daft," she said, as she let him in.

"Well, thank yew darling," grinned Pete, and they both laughed.

It was strange. They hardly knew each other seventeen years ago, but suddenly they were as warm and comfortable as old friends.

He walked into the kitchen ahead of her on a mutual quest for glasses and a vase for the flowers. Ann felt herself smiling. Ready to giggle at the turn of events. She knew this was mostly the effect of Pete's famous irresistible grin and a general feeling of excitement.

Neither said a word until they were both sitting down with the wine. Pete spoke first.

"Here's a toast to a lovely little dolly bird who's turned into a beautiful elegant woman," he said. He was sincere and she knew it. She just raised her glass, nodding her thanks.

"Bet you didn't think I noticed you, but I did. You were Tarquin's girl, and at that time I pretended not to be, but I was a bit in awe of the upper class lads in our circle."

"And you had a large supply of dollies to get through."

"No, my roving eye didn't get into action until after Madeleine."

"And speaking of Madeleine."

"Yeah. That's why I'm here."

"How much did she tell you?"

"Not a lot. I only arrived at your doorstep because I found out where you work by a fluke, and they gave me your address. She never mentioned you. My well-meaning staff did all the sleuthing on their own, nosing into the situation, and found the whereabouts of that bastard, sorry I expect he's a friend of yours."

"So you know where to find him?"

"Already been round there but he seems to be out."

Ann gasped and stared at him. He picked up on her reaction and cocked his head. Waiting for her to say something.

"Well you couldn't have arrived on a better day."

"Okay then, fill up our glasses. Mind if I take off my shoes?"

He didn't wait for an answer, and when she came back with the bottle he was lodged into the sofa cushions in a lotus position, relaxed and calm.

"Griffin…that's what we call him now…is a nutcase on a scale even you might be surprised to know. In his defense, he's been in a physical and emotional state of growing paranoia for many years, and today I think he finally cracked."

Pete hooded his eyes and smiled mysteriously, waiting for her to go on.

"He pulled a gun on some guy he thought was an FBI agent. Turned out he was right, and the same man was just here looking for him, along with a swat team outside his house.."

"Did they get him?"

"No, he's on permanent alert. He's amazing."

"Where is he now?"

"What do you want to do to him?"

"Just talk. The anger's gone, I'm having a good life, and it sounds like he's not. But that's not just the reason. The whole nightmare has to be ended, we need a last chapter. It's more of an intellectual thing than emotional after all these years. I'd like to wrap it up. Also for my friend Barry Turnbull, remember him? He's really damaged goods. I hate that American word closure, so glib, but it's fairly appropriate here."

"I understand. I think it's a good idea for you. It's not going to work for him. He needs to escape, or die."

"So where is he?"

CHAPTER 53

Ann took a long time answering, turning the wine glass in her hand, thinking about her responsibility to both these men, one in the past and one surely in the future.

"Down the hall, in my friend's place."

Pete unraveled himself from the lotus with agility and stood up.

"I want to see him."

"That's up to him. He'll freak when he sees you. I have to talk to him, might take a while."

"Sure, if you say he's that paranoid."

"It's worse than that. He thinks the FBI guy turned up out of nowhere because you reported him."

"Course I didn't, I never would have thought of doing that. It was either pretend I'd never heard about Madeleine meeting him, or make an effort to have a face to face. Which is why I'm here."

"Something happened. It couldn't just be a coincidence."

"Is he carrying a gun?"

"Probably."

"Get it off him before I go in there."

Ann's eyes flashed with defiance.

"You're not going 'in there'. And don't give me orders."

Ann brushed past him and went to the kitchen, letting the broken mood settle between them. She sensed it was an important moment in this new relationship, establishing right away that she wasn't a compliant female. If he didn't like it, then too bad, it was good to find out so quickly.

She decided to give him another chance, and took some fresh wine out of the fridge, marching back into the room with the bottle and an opener, which she placed in front of him. As she hoped, he was ready to speak first.

"I apologize. I've got so used to being bossy at home. There's nobody to stand up to me. Can we go back to the bit where I said, I want to see him?"

"I'd like to go back first to the bit about the good life you're having. Tell me more."

"Well, I was partly lying. I have a great life, beautiful house, comfortable family around me, my old buddy from school, Tony, and his mum that is. They do everything to spoil me rotten and sometimes I think they're happier than I am. My music's doing great, and I'll never worry about money or my place in the world of fame any more, I'm set for life with that."

"Aren't you married anymore?"

"No, I think my timing's been really bad. And because of who I am I get a lot of girls coming at me for the wrong reasons. Seems none of them knows who I am, maybe it's because they don't know who I was. You'd be surprised how important that is. They're all too young, don't laugh, I know it's the male myth, but they can be really boring you know. The Doobies wrote a great song about that. It cuts down the good chat when you can't use all the references."

"You must have a current girlfriend."

"Yes I do, and that sort of sums it up. She's a darling little thing, Asian, waits on me hand and foot, listens patiently to everything I say, does my accounts, that's one of her better tricks."

Ann's smile twitched at his honesty.

Pete's voice wandered off and he stared into his wine for a while.

"But I might as well be completely alone, honestly."

"Yes, you are being honest, Pete."

"Yeah, there's a reason."

"Go on."

"I've been thinking about you ever since I heard you'd met up with Madeleine. I'd like to spend some time with you, get to know each other. We have a background, a kind of bond, don't you think?"

"Well," started Ann, not knowing if there was an answer to this. She found herself liking the idea. She certainly liked him, he felt so familiar too.

"Okay, I'll be really honest then, it was my first priority when I decided to come here. Number one was to meet you. Then came trying to get together with you know who. Then there are a couple of business things, a movie maybe, and some record company guys. But it was the idea of seeing that shy little blonde that really got me going. And that's the truth, I swear. I'll show you my To Do list. I'm a chronic list maker," he grimaced.

"Me too!" laughed Ann, and they both knew something was happening between them. Pete got up and stepped over to Ann in the chair. Then taking her hands, he guided Ann to her feet and put his arms round her.

"Let's have a hug to celebrate," said Pete.

They fitted together with ease, as if they were coming home. They both knew a kiss was the next natural move, and that was the confirmation. But Ann was the first to break it gently, looking into his eyes and smiling.

"I think it would be a good idea to interrupt this now and go to Number 2 on your list."

Pete laughed.

"Okay, you're right, but I'll be thinking all the time of going right back to where we just left off. Tell me you feel the same and I'll let you go."

"I do feel the same, it's good."

CHAPTER 54

When Ann got to her front door she turned round to look at Pete.

"This might take a while, it's just that I'll be waking him up then laying this bombshell on him. He'll need convincing that you're not here to kill him."

When Ann walked into her friend's apartment she put on all the lights and purposely made lots of noise while preparing coffee in the kitchen, then knocked on the bedroom door. Nothing. She knocked again, louder.

Griffin snorted, then gasped as he came to life.

"Fuck. Where the hell am I?"

"Hi Griffin, it's okay, it's Ann. I've made you some coffee."

Ann placed the tray with the pot, sugar and cream, on the bedside table and poured a cup for him. Looking at him with deep sympathy, thinking what the hell have I done to him. This drama all happened because of me, bringing Madeleine over. Griffin looked so alien and Pete seemed so familiar. Little flashes of joy intermingled with other thoughts.

"Griffin, I've got something important to tell you. Come on, why don't you get up and come sit in the kitchen. Bring the coffee."

Five minutes later Ann realized he wasn't coming, and went back to the bedroom to check. He was fast asleep again, coffee untouched, lying on his back and snoring.

She returned to her apartment, slightly relieved at the reprieve, and found Pete lying back on the sofa reading one of her books. He looked up.

"I can't wake him up," she said. "I'll go back in half an hour. How about some snacks?"

She was just placing some cheese, crackers and olives on a plate when she heard a tapping at the front door; it opened. Griffin stood in the open doorway with the cup of coffee in his hand, staring in absolute shock at Pete Stebbings.

CHAPTER 55

Pete Stebbings stared back. Hatred spilled from his eyes.

Pete broke the spell.

"'allo Leo you old bastard. How're you doin'?"

Griffin plonked himself down opposite Ann, looking at her, puzzled and vague, waiting for her to say something, ignoring the phantom Pete.

"Griffin. Here's the bottom line. Pete Stebbings is here."

"Are you shitting me? Ann, did you plan this?"

"No, and first of all he didn't report you to the FBI, nobody did. Madeleine told him she'd met you and he wasn't interested, but his friend Barry was, and somehow his assistant tracked you down. It sounds like Pete's forgiven you, his life is good, and....."

"And, like I told Ann, I just want to heal the past now. What about you, man, you look bloody awful. Is this what vengeance looks like?"

Griffin drained the cup empty and focused his bleary eyes on the apparition in front of him. Then he wiped his mouth with the back of his hand and tried to speak, clearing his throat as a cover for his complete discomfort.

"I don't really know what it looks like. And how can I believe you weren't responsible for bringing the law down on me?"

"Well you can't. Because I can vow it wasn't me personally, but I do believe that somehow my conscientious minders must have walked into a few old tripwires that had been set up around you by the law in their quest to track you down. And that was not so much for me, not specifically anyway, but more because of our old friend Barry Turnbull, remember him? He went off the rails when he heard you were still around. He's been wanting to dismember you since lily law walked in that night. He knew you set us up, an animal instinct he has, and you fucked up his life. I have to tell you, he's a basket case just staying this side of suicide by a sacrificing wife and a shitload of pharmaceuticals. How do you feel about that, King Leo, Acid Guru to the Stars?"

Griffin winced and averted his eyes.

"Aren't you going to tell us why the FBI is so interested in you after this many years? It wasn't just because you were their dealer, and you didn't fail in your mission, not the first one anyway, you certainly did away with The Veils and turned a generation of kids on to acid, eh? What's the rest of your story, Leo?"

Griffin let out a huge sigh, turning up pleading eyes.

"I just went through that with Ann. My confession, I mean. Do I have to do it again? Right now? Please, Ann, you tell him. I'm out of words."

"Suits me, Leo, I'll listen to Ann telling me any kind of story."

Ann leaned over to Pete and laid her hand on his arm. Then she thought better of that idea, got up and sat close to him, linking her arm through his. They exchanged a look of complicity, with Griffin's face becoming even more miserable before she spoke again.

"I'll fill him in with the story up to the point where you left off, Griffin. Where you said you took a file, they never found it, then you escaped. What did you do, create your own witness protection program?"

Griffin couldn't help but chuckle.

"You've got the imagination, that's for sure. Yeah, I did some traveling as Gary Willet, the name you saw on my phone bill that time. Got all the papers lined up, tried the rural recluse bit, too obvious, so I decided to hide in plain sight right here in this great city, just as it was getting crowded with international nefarious types and the usual bums, then I found this wacky environment. Perfect for me until now. I gave up trying to get a passport without setting off flares, and I thought I was safe."

"Yes, that's the point, isn't it Griffin? Safe from what? There's a bottom line here you haven't got to yet. I can understand that you're a threat because of what you know, from the file. But what else did you do?"

Griffin sat there in stony silence, knowing that eyes were boring into him.

"You know me too well."

"Yes. I know if you think it's so bad you can't talk about it, it can only mean one thing."

"Come on, Leo. We've got a train to catch," snapped Pete.

"It was an accident. More like self-defense."

"Here it comes," said Ann softly.

"An FBI man, I suppose," added Pete helpfully.

"Yes, he was the night minder. I'd planned everything perfectly. On my way out of the door for good, middle of the night. I wasn't meant to run into him. He'd gone to the toilet. He came right at me, swinging a baseball bat. That's all they did, the minders, practice their swings. We had a stupid tussle, and his gun was holstered but I knew he'd grab it the first opportunity. I just wanted to live. I got hold of the bat and just hit him once, only once I promise you. More strength than I knew I had, it was the passion in me. I thought later in a court of law I could have got off with a light sentence, but hey, there was no justice coming up for me. Just once and he was gone, his skull was just…like…..Sorry."

There was no rejoinder, no comforting remark, no witty riposte, just dead air in the room. Pete broke the silence.

"You're going to have to answer for it, Leo. No use running. The court of law is waiting for you, man."

"They want to kill me. This is no official search. Why do you think that FBI guy is under cover? When he finds me he'll shoot me stone dead. Unless he's got some plan to take me somewhere and torture me first. That's if they still want that file."

"You still got it?"

"Security deposit box. I've set it up, anything happens to me, the key will be found, unleash the dogs of war. That stuff will never be redundant."

"Griffin's got a point. The man didn't have a card, he just wrote a phone number on a piece of paper with his last name only, Cortez."

"Why should you get away with murder?"

"It was him or me. Put yourself in my shoes, at that time, I mean."

"No thanks. I'm beginning to see the attraction of being a washed up rock star with a criminal record. You put yourself in your shoes,

Leo. You made it happen. What the hell were you doing breaking us young kids with your drug scam? Was it to have the power, hang out with the trendies, be the Acid King for a few glorious weeks or something, get the birds fascinated with your mysterious façade?"

"All the above. And more. I got caught myself, with hash and homemade acid coming in to London. I was such a skillful joker I almost got away with it, but I got the attention of the customs guys, and then the airport security man, who put me in a room to present to a few of his colleagues, until the head man walked in. He was serious level. Not CID, probably MI5 or 6, I never found out. He was one of those toffee nosed bastards, as you would call him, definitely a big shot. He kept asking me questions, nodding and thinking up a storm behind that polite attitude. They must have had some plan, and I was just what they were looking for." Griffin skewered Pete with a look that begged sympathy.

"You remember the times, Pete. The authorities kept knocking off the odd musician, Donovan, Brian Jones, but they were looking for a big scoop. They took me to a lock up, and a couple of days later in walks the big man accompanied by the American equivalent of him. After a couple of meaningless remarks, he made me a proposition. Offered me complete freedom, not even a plea bargain, nothing on my record. All I had to do was follow instructions."

Griffin looked at his audience just to check they were still following him. He didn't need to. Pete was absorbing every word.

"To the letter. They explained the whole thing but refused to write it down. I had to memorize and repeat the program. They would provide me with all the drugs, highest quality, a mixture of hash, grass of various vintages, including some new ones. Man these people were clearly in the racket. Columbia, Peru, Humboldt County, you name it, the best, all packaged brilliantly. And their *pièce de résistance* was the acid. They explained it was the most pure, liquid, hospital stuff. That fixed it for me, I knew they had to be CIA. They'd practically invented the stuff. Now they were ready to put it on the market in a blaze of publicity, to coin a phrase."

"So what was their plan?" asked Pete with flinty eyes and a nasty look.

"I just had to launch myself into society. Spin a web of enchantment with free drugs. The charming Yank who became the darling of the swinging set, zero in on the most famous ones and bring 'em down baby. You happened to be first. But it got out of hand, I didn't have a chance to incriminate my next victims. The damage was done. I had to run for it."

Pete's expression sagged into a picture of nostalgia and regret.

Ann was quietly crying.

"But you know what really almost caught them with their pants down? It was Madeleine, that beautiful girl, I would have done anything to have a romance with her, I worshipped Madeleine. The way she suffered made the whole crappy deal look pathetic, even though they got what they wanted. The man who was my supervisor on the deal, the one who whisked me away from the scene and out of London, he was screaming at me, blaming me for including the girl in the bust. 'I didn't plan on having no damn Joan of Arc to contend with here', he yelled, spitting all over me. They went soft on their tactics after that, reasonably satisfied with the chaos they'd created, until they had to face up to John Lennon later on, he was the really serious spanner in the works for them. He never let up. God bless his soul."

Griffin looked at the mess he had made, and decided to continue.

"So there I was, back in the States, in a safe house, ha ha, next best thing to prison in fact, no passport, and too dangerous to let go. A grenade with a loose pin, and foaming at the mouth in my usual way. What were they going to do with me? I was their loose cannon. I reckoned I was a one bullet option. Nobody knew who I was or where I'd gone, only my mother cared. My father had been dead for a year, and my sister didn't give a damn about me, I was the deadbeat sibling long before that happened, hippie freak and all that, closest thing to Manson she knew in her little anal corporation world."

There was no reaction to him.

"You appreciate, I hope, that no one in this life has heard this whole story. I've kept the whole experience zipped up in my gut somewhere, like a nasty little devil I have to feed with booze, weed, coke and questionable food. Except for Juno, that is. And she's never heard it like this. She still thinks she can save me. She tried to make me normal with a child, but it didn't hold up to its looming father figure. After that I never let her try any more. I married her because of the pregnancy and to keep her loyal."

CHAPTER 56

"What do you want now, Leo? What is it?" Pete asked.

"Escape. A ticket to Mexico, that's just the jumping off point, a passport, then down into cocaine land. I'll disappear. Live like a peasant. I long for it. Start again, be at peace."

For the first time since he got there Pete looked at his watch, and his compulsive list-making mind shot into gear.

"Ann, I hope you don't mind, I have to make a phone call, there's someone on my mind now I have to get in touch with. I'll make it short."

CHAPTER 57

In the kitchen Pete checked his phone list for the number he wanted, dialing it, long distance.

The ringing droned on for a while before Carol's pinched voice answered with a hello that had a quivering question mark at the end of it.

"Hi, Carol, it's Pete, I'm in Los Angeles."

"Oh Thank God! Have you seen him?"

" Who?"

"Barry. He'll be there in L.A. by now, tricky little bastard. He left without telling me, I was out, then he called with a message from the airport…"

"Slow down, Carol. Why is he in L.A.? I thought he was too wigged out to cross the fucking road."

"I don't know why, Pete, but I know how. You gave him the money."

"Oh shit. I did but that wasn't the idea. Crafty blighter, but did he give you any idea who he was planning to see, anything like that?"

" I can tell you this, from the sound of his voice he's taken a few days' worth of his happy pills. I'm worried about him. I'm really scared, Pete. What are we going to do?"

"Let me talk to a few people. Like Tony, find out if Barry called him, if he knows I'm here and where to find me. Listen, I'm at the Mondrian, Tony's got the number, but call him if you hear anything, he'll leave a message if I'm not in my room, and I'll get straight back to you. Let you know if he turns up."

"Promise, Pete?"

"Sure, Carol. I promise."

Pete shook his head as blinding calculations whizzed through his brain. He dialed his home number to reach Tony, drumming his fingers on the tiles. He knew there'd be a swift pickup and he rode over Tony's formal voice.

"Listen, Tony, this is urgent. Did Barry call you in the last couple of days?"

There was slight hesitation before he said, "No. Why?"

"Because he got on a plane and flew over here, that's why. Anything I should know? Like, that address you gave me on the dealer..."

"Oh Christ. Yeah man. I told Carol, but she would never tell him anything like that."

"He must have got hold of it somehow. We're in trouble here, Tony."

"Let me call that friend of mine, you know, the security guy I got the info from. What about the girl?"

"What girl?"

"Madeleine's friend. She might know something. She works at that free weekly paper."

"Yes I know," said Pete with irritation now at being outpaced.

"So later, then, chief," said Tony hanging up hastily.

CHAPTER 58

"Something's wrong," said Ann, looking at him as he put the phone down and came back into the room. Pete glared at Griffin.

"Barry's in L.A. and my guess is he'll be over at your place waiting for you."

"Not possible."

"Really? I'd already been over there myself, before I came here," said Pete.

Griffin perked up.

"Were the cops still there?"

"Not a sign. I walked around, cased the place, knocked a few times, it was real quiet."

"I gotta go over. Something I left behind. Be right back."

"Don't be crazy, Griffin. They'll be watching for you."

Griffin disappeared. Ann knew what he was doing.

"Pete, you know the police'll jump on him the second he appears."

"Yes, I've seen that on the telly. And I did notice there were a lot of new cars parked around for such a dump. What do you reckon he left there?"

"Probably that key. Pete we have to go with him."

"Not you, darling."

Ann firmed up. "I'm coming," she said.

Griffin walked back into the apartment in his full rabbi gear. Pete just shook his head.

"You're too much, man. Is this the way you have to live?"

"Goes with my nose, don't you think?"

He opened the coat and revealed a glimpse of his gun, a big smile to go with it.

"Yes, this is the way I live."

He wheeled around and disappeared so quickly that Pete and Ann had to scramble to follow him. By the time they'd made it to the street all they could see was a pair of tail-lights vanishing ahead.

"My car's right here. We know where he's going," Pete called out. Ann didn't hesitate.

Seated in the car and strapping in, Ann looked over.

"Please don't tell me you're enjoying yourself."

"Huh? Me?"

"Good to be alive, isn't it?"

Pete leaned over to kiss her on the cheek but suddenly oncoming headlights blinded him. He watched as Cortez jammed his brakes, jumped out of the car and ran over to them.

"You alright, Miss Stapleton?" he asked, peering across Pete and into Ann's startled eyes. Then without waiting for an answer. "I'd like to talk to both of you."

"Have you heard anything from Griffin?" asked Ann sincerely.

"My man on duty down the street told me a unidentified car has been parked here for several hours...."

"Griffin doesn't have a car," Ann replied "Not what you would call a car, he does have a wrecked looking jeep I've never seen him drive."

Cortez looked angry.

"That thing is still parked near his residence. I'm talking about the car that just left. My officer said it went off in that direction."

"Must have been visiting one of my neighbors," Ann said, concerned about what Barry would do if he was hanging about outside waiting for Griffin when he pulled up.

"Well, if you don't mind, then, I'd like to take Miss Stapleton to dinner," said Pete politely. He knew they were trapped, and even when they got away there was a good chance the agent would follow them, but it was all a risk now. His priority was Barry, and the hope that he wouldn't unleash the rage he'd bottled up for years at the sight of his enemy.

***

When they saw that Cortez was following them, and making no effort to conceal it, Pete and Ann headed straight for Le Dome and swung to the right into the hands of the valet parking attendants. They could see Cortez slow down, then stop and double park ahead of the restaurant. He sat for a while and waited. Watching Pete and Ann enter arm-in-arm. Then decided to head back to the stake-out in the hope that Rivkin would appear.

Ann and Pete went downstairs and left through the back exit. Collected the car, and drove off.

CHAPTER 59

Griffin's Place

It was dark as Griffin the rabbi came loping round the block and walked past the alleyway entrance, his eyes flitting in all directions, looking for signs of watchers, in cars, on rooftops. He circled the entire block and came back the other way, checking out the street door, then moved round to the back entrance, stopped, looked each way, slipped in his key and stepped inside.

At the foot of the stairs he stopped and looked around. There was a small light burning at his desk just as he left it and he went straight there to case its contents, checking out the hidden drawer and seeing it hadn't been disturbed. Groping under the drawer space, he tore off something that was taped down, a key inside a plastic envelope. Took off the hat, wig and overcoat, mopped his brow with the scarf and tossed it on the chair. Only then did he look into the far corner of the room straight down the barrel of Barry's gun.

"Who the fuck are you?" snapped Griffin, keeping it together like an old pro. Barry switched on the light beside his chair.

"Just an old drug buddy from the sixties, King Leo."

"Jesus," said Griffin, genuinely amazed, "Barry, from The Veils. What is this, Top of the Pops? Just been chatting to old Pete Stebbings. What next, the Jim and Jimi show?"

"No, chum, they're dead. Me, I'm one of the living dead. Thanks to you, you bastard. And I've only been living for this moment."

"Mind if I sit down, then, so we talk about it?

Without waiting for an answer Griffin sat down on his desk chair, where he'd dropped his overcoat, knowing exactly how to reach the pocket with the gun in it, and thinking about the when.

"What's to discuss, your fucking majesty?".

"Your friend Pete was fascinated enough to discuss our mutual history for an hour or so. Don't you want to hear the details before you zip my mouth?"

"I've got one question for you."

"Only one, after all this time?"

"Who were you working for?"

"Cointelpro. Ever heard of that?"

"No."

"And I thought you were such an alert political little beast."

Barry didn't rise to the bait. His voice was calm.

"Who is Cointelpro?"

"It's a snappy name for an FBI counter intelligence program. Object was to eliminate radicals, whatever it took. You guys were a pushover, a few nights in jail and you turned into mush, crying, committing suicide, nervous breakdowns, heroin, they knew you didn't have the guts to actually take up the political sword and fight them back. You sang a good song, but you were all weak as baby shit when your plush little rock star lives were threatened. Did you know you could have won if you'd pushed back? You had the numbers, man, look at Woodstock. That had the governments worried. They don't like those numbers, it brings out the worst in them. Look what they did after all those gay studs rioted in San Francisco." He sighed with nostalgia.

"What did they do after San Francisco?"

"AIDS, man, AIDS, where the hell do you think it came from? They had it in Africa first, cooked up in the alphabet soup kitchen, CIA, NSA, FBI, like all the other plans brewing in there, new world odor, man, you can smell it coming. You think all those black skeletal folk are just starving, no man they're sick."

He paused, noticing Barry's hand relaxing its grip of the gun.

"Give these big government guys another twenty years and it's gonna be too late to look back and say Oh Yeah, I see. We all let it happen, me too, except I was just too beaten up and solitary to do anything with it. A whole generation gave up the fight and now we're all battery chickens, so much for flower power, that sick fuck Charlie Manson gave the conservatives a big boost and they took it from there, it was all over. We got neutralized, man, that's just the kind of word they like in the service. Sounds clean and effective, looks good on paper. The sixties revolution was neutralized."

Griffin pierced Barry with his steel blue eyes.

"Yeah, when you guys shopped for drugs, you made it look edgy and smart, even getting caught became a trend, so all the little mouths were open, tongues out, gimme some of that acid, let's all drift away, stop crying about Kennedy, quit fretting about Vietnam, blanking out the nightmares, what a cruel scam, you bought the whole trip, and your followers went with you, into the seventies, lipstick and eye shadow, glitz and sham, rock and roll, free and easy sex, backstage glam. You got maneuvered out of your right to say no to the way your world was being organized. None of you got into parliament, or congress, you let the straights do that for you."

"The career professionals, they're here, they're not going away and they get more powerful with every administration. Watch 'em. They were getting into position in the sixties and seventies while you were all prancing around feeling sorry for yourselves and sucking up cocaine. Millions of you, getting hung up with consuming all the goodies, dumb movies, crass TV, violence for fun, the sports racket, victims of your own lazy greed. All being manipulated into mass stupidity, not even bothering to vote. You lot are wankers, your word, man, suits you perfectly." Griffin let it sink in with a pause, noting that Barry was wilting under attack.

"Well, maybe not all of you. John Lennon tried hard enough, but he got turned into a sideshow, there's so many ways of neutralizing the troublemakers, apart from shooting them. Then they shoot anyway, there's too much paperwork piling up, agents have other suckers to watch. Yeah, like me, good old Lennie, The Acid King, His Highness King Leo, fucking con man for the shop, only the best drugs for the stars, who loved me. It was a brief and glorious time, I was a free spirit, so they locked me up. Eight years of it, witness protection they called it, like living in a cage."

"You're still living in a cage."

"Compared to what? Freedom? Compared to who, you, Barry?"

"Fuck you," he said, but there was no energy in his words.

"Here," said Griffin. "For old time's sake."

Slowly he reached into his pocket and brought out a pipe, filled it with pot from a small can, and tamped it down before passing it across to Barry with a lighter in one smooth gesture.

"You need to relax."

"I don't do that shit anymore."

"That's your problem, Barry. Solve it. Take one hit. You remember how to do that."

Barry lit the pipe and sucked in a tentative mouthful. He held his breath for a long time, watching Griffin watching him.

Slowly letting go he croaked, "You're a crazy motherfucker, Leo, you really believe all that stuff."

"Hell no, just made it up."

He watched Barry carefully, seeing that in spite of the smoke he was still firmly holding the gun in a ready position, although his arm was resting now across his knees.

"Oh, you mustn't leave without looking at an old photograph. It's on the wall behind you."

Barry smirked. "I'm not leaving until I've done you."

"Sure man, I'll be dead but at least you'll know where the photograph is. Interesting to see how you've completely lost your looks, but I still recognized you immediately. Did you keep your voice, I hope? You could sing, that's a sure thing, better than your friend, but you knew that, it made you angry."

Barry was starting to lose his composure, the gun weaving in his hand.

"Shut up, Leo."

The moment was shattered by the sound of thumping at the door. Then Pete Stebbings' voice, calling out for Griffin to let him in.

In one of three cars parked at strategic locations around the building, a plainclothes cop was barking into the radio.

"Agent Cortez?"

"Right here."

"That unknown who entered the suspect's property. We identified him. Barry Turnbull, an Englishman, suspect knows him…"

"What? How'd you know that?"

"Seems the rabbi we were tracking must be the suspect. He's inside too."

"What? You're not making sense. What are you seeing?"

"A man and a woman. Going in."

"I'm on my way."

CHAPTER 60

Griffin rose carefully, holding his arms up to Barry.

"Hold it now, Barry. We have to let them in, don't we?"

He backed towards the door, opened it and stood aside to let Pete in. Ann followed and closed the door. She stood beside Pete, who spoke calmly.

"Okay Barry, I admit it's a great idea and you've been thinking about it for years, but I suggest you give it some more thought, like, prison again? Eh? And what about Carol, she's waiting for my call to tell her that her beloved Barry is alive and well and not doing something stupid."

Equally calm, Griffin stepped behind Ann and ushered her into the main area of the tiny space. He came close to the door, and Barry reacted immediately, lifting the gun and pointing it with a very steady hand.

"You're not going anywhere mate. Get away from that door."

"Just checking. We don't want anyone walking in, do we?"

Griffin gave the door a solid push and bolted it with a piece of wood. But he didn't move too far. Close enough now to the rifle hooked overhead, invisible in the dark corner above the door. Griffin spread his arms in a benevolent gesture.

"This is historic. The three of us together again, honoring my little hovel in apocalyptic L.A. The last time was in an English country manor when the world was prosperous and inspiring."

"Yeah," snarled Barry, "I remember."

"So why don't we all take a stroll round the corner and have a drink together. I don't have much of a bar here."

"Yeah, we can discuss our karma," Barry snarled.

"Exactly what I had in mind. We have a bond now. Sudden death by bullets is beneath us. We have a higher call. Look at how much our world has changed, and we've all survived it."

"What do you think I am, bloody stupid? Or an infant?"

"No, Barry, I'm just trying to stop you killing me."

"Well, you can spin out the time as much as you like, but I'm gonna do it anyway."

Inside the van where the surveillance tape crackled, Cortez was quietly cursing himself. He felt almost out of his depth. In all his years of service he'd never encountered anything like this. Perhaps it was because these people were not conventional criminals. That maniac Rivkin had led him a dance all day, he clenched his teeth as he realized that one of those rabbis he'd encountered had been him, the bastard. He must have stared straight into his face.

On top of that, a woman had clearly outsmarted him. Thanks to the cop on watch outside Ann's apartment, he knew that Pete Stebbings had been in there with her for hours. Now here was someone called Barry, who was carrying a weapon.

He'd considered blocking off the exit to the alley but thought better of it. He desperately wanted to rush the place with all his men, guns blazing, but that wasn't the answer either. So he sat in this shabby corner of a city he was getting to hate, listening to the electronic surveillance sounds of a bunch of lunatics.

***

Griffin was using the time to scan around for hidden mics or cameras. He was sure the Feds had rigged up something, and he knew they must be outside there choking over what they were hearing.

Without making any sudden moves, he sauntered over to his sound system and pulled out an audio tape from a box.

"It seems a good moment to play you something which we'll all enjoy," he said, punching in the cassette. Out came an old blues song which Pete and Barry had recorded together many years before, a live club performance, and obviously a pirate tape.

"Where'ja get that?" asked Pete.

"See what I mean, Barry?" Griffin said. That was 1965. I was there. Pete was good but you were better."

Griffin took a slow step back, lifted his right arm and quietly unhooked the rifle from its place high up on the wall. In the same smooth movement he brought it up, opened the safety catch with a nasty click and held it to Pete's head.

"Wasn't he Pete?"

CHAPTER 61

Barry was taken by surprise, and Pete had both hands showing in a pacifying defensive gesture as he slowly leaned over and removed the gun from Barry's fingers. Placing it on the floor, out of reach. Ann sat there with her arms folded, meeting Pete's eyes as if they offered some kind of security.

"I don't want any dialogue," Griffin said. "Just understand this. They've got this place wired and with the music they can't hear me. I don't want to hurt any of you, but I will if I have to."

He glanced over all their faces, keeping the rifle steady.

"Now, Barry, what've you got in your pocket? Hand it to me."

Barry stared forlornly at Griffin, before shuffling himself around to reach into the back of his pants, pulling out wallet and keys.

"And your passport?"

Barry looked over at Pete, who shrugged at him.

"Hey, it's a robbery, you'll get another one."

Griffin checked for cash, saw enough to make his eyes twinkle, then flipped through the passport, checking the photo.

"It'll do. On a bad day I can look like this."

He grinned at them. The irony was that the two boys were singing joyfully in the background.

"Now. You'll all step outside and get in Pete's little rental, with this piece right on his cranium, and I'll direct you to where we're going. Pete, you'll drive, and the three of us will be all hunched up in the back seat, so there won't be any nice easy shots for the snipers. Sorry to do this to you, Ann, you're a good lady. It should be Madeleine, but she just has that lucky charm."

He held up a finger to his lips, as he bent carefully to lift Barry's gun from the floor. Then picked up his overcoat from the chair, sliding one arm at a time into the coat, while pocketing Barry's gun.

"No dialogue, no quick moves, no resistance. You are now hostages, so act the part and no one gets hurt. On your feet. Keep your arms up high in the air. Ann, you're in charge of Barry, nothing stupid please. You go first and open up the door, go easy."

CHAPTER 62

The frustration on the faces of Cortez and the others outside was suddenly replaced by urgency and shock. They'd been sitting through what seemed to be the longest loudest rock and roll anthem ever. Now the door opened and Ann came out with her hands in the air, followed by the two men, and Rivkin holding a rifle to the head of one of them. It was a horrible sight.

"Jesus, that's a semi-automatic." The undercover detective sitting next to Cortez said.

"Get the word out. Do nothing. The hostages are not struggling, they're all too close together. If your best sniper can get a shot in his head, do it, but no, cancel that, they're getting into a car. That's Stebbings' rental. We'll follow it, stay close enough but easy does it. I don't want to provoke him, this guy is on the edge, nothing to lose, okay? No sirens." He sounded calmer than he felt. Cortez realized he had unleashed a potential international tragedy and he was frightened at the enormity of it.

The detective repeated his instructions over the transmitter. What Cortez didn't want to think about was the report he was going to have to write if it all blew up in his face. And how he would explain that his little vacation to Florida was a lie. Not one that could be justified by this fiasco playing out in the busy streets of L.A.

"They're heading west, lot of traffic, but we won't lose 'em," the voice on the transmitter assured.

"Bloody Troubadour?" blasted Pete from the driver's seat. "What for?"

"Great show on there tonight, I want you two boys to have a good time," Griffin answered.

CHAPTER 63

The Toyota slowed down in the heavy traffic on Santa Monica Boulevard as it approached the club, and slipped into the alleyway leading to the back.

"Hey, look who's playing, I know them," Barry said, looking at the marquee.

"We're going straight to the bar. Stay close, act nice and friendly," snapped Griffin firmly.

Tell the valet to park the car across the road on Doheny, facing south, and give him this," Griffin continued.

The busy valets identified Pete Stebbings, nodding as he gave the nearest one Griffin's twenty-dollar bill, straight from Barry's wallet.

The valet jumped into Pete's car, backed up and zoomed away before the first of Cortez's follow up cars came into view.

***

The group walked into the club, and again Griffin flashed the money to pay their cover charge, but immediately Pete was recognized. Happy faces and back-slapping, hand-clasping fan worship escorted them in, and the two musicians couldn't help but surrender. Landing at the bar, Griffin's eyes were flicking around, expecting the suits to walk in any minute.

"Wanta jam with the guys?" asked a roadie, gesturing to the band onstage, playing rock and roll in the traditional seventies groove. Pete knew the roadie and the band, who'd been around for years, and he wanted to say yes, but he looked quickly at Griffin for a reaction.

"Great idea, do it, man," said Griffin, all magnanimous and warm as if he were some kind of manager, with just a casual pat on the right hand pocket of his jacket, a subtle reminder of the gun inside.

"Follow me," said the roadie, and they all four surged after him through the thick crowd, many of them nodding and patting Pete on the back, one guy shouting above the noise. "Hey, it's Barry Turnbull, this is great. The two of them together. This is history, this is cool!"

Up on the stage the usual easy deferential procedure between musicians went on as Pete modestly sashayed over to the lead singer, nudging him and grinning, starting roars from the crowd, graciously accepting a mic and hitting straight into a blues yell, the guitars picking up steam with renewed energy. Just behind him Barry came on stage more hesitantly, joined Pete at the mic, gingerly harmonizing in the song, then picking up momentum as Pete grinned at him, put his arm around Barry's shoulder and brought him closer to the shared mic. The band bounced and smirked with the infectious boost in crowd reaction, and at the edge of the stage Ann looked up, as all the years rolled away, and she forgot about the pain and confusion, and even the last few hours.

A roadie navigated the crowded stage and slipped another mic into Barry's hand, as he got into a full deep blues roar and started to take over. The crowd was in heaven, waving their arms and whooping with every rising syllable. For Pete and Barry, after nearly eighteen years, this was a sudden and magical reunion. Pete wanted to make sure Ann knew she was part of it as he looked down and gave her a special grin.

All too high to notice the two suits pushing to the front of the stage and fanning around each side, joined by two more.

CHAPTER 64

The rental car was located next morning close to Rivkin's place, so the puzzle was magnified. Cortez was even more mired in the mess, with a deep gut feeling that once again he had been outwitted by Rivkin.

By the time the late report reached him that Barry's rental had been removed from the parking spot outside Canter's, also close to Rivkin's's place, he knew he had lost. The report included corroborated accounts from all the hostages, including Barry's reason for taking three days to return to his car. They were celebrating their reunion at Pete's hotel, he said. It added up. Cortez had been conned. Rivkin's cunning had secured him a passport, money, two guns, a semi-automatic and an unidentifiable car. When it turned up in Mexico City three weeks later, innocently parked in a huge mall, it was too late. Griffin had disappeared again.

Calvin Cortez, the self-anointed smooth operator, had met his match.

CHAPTER 65

Ann's Apartment

As soon as she could find time away from Pete, who was meeting the movie people for lunch, Ann dialed Madeleine's number, hoping she'd be there. She was almost exploding with the news and didn't want to leave any messages. Madeleine's coolly amused voice at the other end of the line was just the antidote she needed after the madness, and in a whirl of excitement, relief and Madeleine's hungry questions, the vivid story came flying out.

"So you missed all the action," Ann said when she thought she'd finished.

"No. I did what I had to do. I set him up."

"But you didn't plan for the happy ending."

"I got what I needed. I didn't want to kill him, just balance the books." She hesitated. "How do you feel?"

"Like a new life is beginning."

"Are you going to write about it?"

"No. No need for that. The book's closed. I hope Tarquin can rest in peace now. Wait till you see what it's done for Pete and Barry. It was like the cure for cancer overnight."

"Good. I like this feeling too. It could be my next song."

CHAPTER 66

Pete's House – Two Months Later

A party was in progress, the house and spacious gardens were not too crowded, and there was a special celebration vibe on the faces and the fancy clothes. The mood was casual and easy, as always with successful people mingling comfortably with their coterie of personal friends.

Carol and Tony were perched on garden chairs watching the action, sipping on moisture-beaded glasses of Pimms.

"Only Pete would launch a wedding and a new CD on the same day."

"Only Pete would be that intelligent about the economics of it."

Carol smiled at Tony's accurate comment.

"And the bride, bless her, she looks so happy."

He surreptitiously squeezed her thigh, still staring at the crowd.

"Tony! What was that for?"

"I was just remembering Bournemouth, and how you looked."

"Well, you'd better not."

"I'm already planning on Brighton next time."

Carol giggled happily and stuck her face into the Pimm's to cover her blushes.

They both smiled at their expanded family. Barry caught their eyes and waved over, a cloying teenager on each arm, a shameless Cheshire cat look on his face, forehead glistening, hair tousled. He looked slim and fifteen years younger.

The presentation of their CD was close at hand, discreetly displayed for the few exclusive media people who had been invited. Pete was on the other side of one of the blondes, and they were posing for the flashbulbs.

"So how did you actually meet up with Pete in Los Angeles?"

Ann turned from laughing at the boys' antics to answer the journalist.

"Oh, it was a wild coincidence. We just happened to go into the Troubadour the same night, the band was a favorite from the old days, and it was a sudden impulse I had to see them. Great, eh?"

"Lovely, just a coincidence.

"And why was Barry there that night, were they already talking reunion?"

"Oh yes, Barry came for a visit here a week or so before that, and it was discussed. Yes."

"After eighteen years. Just like that?"

"Oh, excuse me, I see someone…"

Madeleine and her daughter were arriving. The teenager was a beauty and there wasn't a person she passed who didn't stop to look. Madeleine headed straight to Ann, taking Charlotte's hand and drawing her along.

"Come say hello to Ann. She likes you so much, lucky girl."

"Can you believe your luck, Charlotte," laughed Madeleine as she kissed Ann on both cheeks. "You've got me and now you've got the most fabulous stepmother in the world."

"Oh, Mum, you're going over the top again."

Boring in on them in a typical tough-skinned media fashion was the same journalist again.

"Er, sorry Mrs. Stebbings, one more thing I didn't get to ask you back there. What happened to the mystery man at the country house?"

"I really don't know. Do you, Madeleine?"

"No, he just seemed to disappear into the woodwork all those years ago, we stopped thinking about him."

Pete broke it up, by calling out loudly.

"Alright now, everybody. Listen up 'cause it's time for a speech from our Best Man before he has too many of those little drinks with umbrellas in 'em. Okay, hands together for Mister Barry Turnbull!!!"

All ongoing conversations stopped as friends and family filled the air with cheers and clapping while Barry bowed, took the mic and filled the stage.

Pete Stebbings glowed with the rightness of it all, in control but feeling complete at last.

***

THE END

ABOUT THE AUTHOR

Maggie Abbott started writing novels when she moved to Palm Springs after a long, successful show business career in Los Angeles, London, Rome, and New York.

A casual job as a secretary at the William Morris Agency in Rome introduced her to the exciting scene of *Cleopatra*, Fellini's *8½* and *The Pink Panther*, with the city's influx of big stars calling by the office every day, and triggered her lifelong love affair with movies.

Over the years, Maggie has enjoyed being in the most interesting places at the best of their times, while working as the movie agent for some exciting stars: Mick Jagger, David Bowie, Charlotte Rampling, Jacqueline Bisset, Martin Sheen, Raquel Welch, Christopher Plummer,

Robert Redford, Mia Farrow, Peter Sellers, Richard Chamberlain, Peter O'Toole, Britt Ekland, Ken Russell, John Boorman, and many more.

Somewhere in between, Maggie was the production assistant on three Broadway plays, and a producer and studio executive at Columbia Pictures where she developed and got production credits on two movies.